D1617123

Calculated Risk

A Blackbridge Security Novel
Marie James

Other Books in the Blackbridge Security Series

Copyright

Synopsis

As the fixer for Blackbridge Security, Quinten Lake is the man that comes in and cleans up after people make stupid decisions.

Which means he didn't want to be the one teaching lustful women gun safety.

There were guys on the team better suited for the task.

Get in and get out, that's his motto, something he lives by not only at work but also in his personal life.

And he could be doing just that if it weren't for the internet.

But if *#BlackbridgeSpecial* weren't trending online, he would've never met Hayden Prescott.

He wouldn't be wondering why she won't make eye contact with him.

He's supposed to teach her the skills to protect herself, but his ego is encouraging him to be her means of protection.

She isn't impressed, and he's left wondering if she'll ever open her eyes and finally see *him*.

Chapter 1

Quinten

"How many?" I ask before Wren hands me the list.

"Fourteen," the Blackbridge IT specialist responds as he digs through a stack of paper on his messy desk.

"There are only seven lanes," I remind him.

"I know," he says with a shrug, but I highly doubt the computer guy has even stepped foot inside of a gun range. "They'll double up. You can learn as much from observing as you can doing a task, and before you make fun of me for not being very proficient in firearms, that goes for nearly everything in life."

I look down at the list when he hands it to me, but I don't really spend much time going over details. There's no way to determine just by a list of names which of these women are in it for the wrong reason.

The goal is to teach women gun safety and how to shoot properly. The problem is, Wren used our company website like a thirst trap for horny women, drawing in over three hundred women for this six-week long class.

"I've picked the women that I felt needed the most help. The online bots I set up flagged those with 911 calls, repeated hospital visits, and women getting restraining orders. That sort of thing."

The simple list in my hand gives none of that information, and I'm actually grateful it doesn't.

I'm the crisis management consultant for Blackbridge Security—the fixer if you will. As such, I do a lot of work with politicians and people in the spotlight when they mess up or have some sort of scandal brewing that could have dire consequences for their public image, which in turn has the ability to ruin their livelihoods.

As the in-house fixer, the less I know about these women, the better. I'm tasked with gun safety, not digging deeper into their lives and eradicating the issue that caused them to need the class in the first place. When I see a problem that I think has a fairly easy solution, I normally steamroll whoever is in the way to fix it. I'm very proficient at my job.

And that begs the question of how I've been the not-so-lucky one to end up teaching this class instead of our weapons expert, Kit Riggs.

"So, like all domestic assaults?" I ask him, because how can I look down at a list of women, knowing they need help and not want to intervene?

"There are a couple in there, but one has a violent brother getting out of prison soon. One woman was in a gang, and they haven't taken too kindly to her leaving that life. A couple more work night shift and have problems on their walks home after work. Three have had recent break-ins, one was even a home invasion. I picked the ones that flagged as needing us the most for this first class."

"First class? This isn't the only class?"

A scoffing sound comes from the corner of the room, but I don't look in that direction. I'm surprised Wren's African Grey parrot is just now making his presence known. The bird has a foul mouth and an attitude problem.

"Deacon mentioned having more than one to meet the need."

I could choke my boss, but being out of a job on a Tuesday morning isn't on my to-do list.

"And none of the other guys offered to help?"

"You're on your own with this one," Wren says as he spins away from me and begins typing quickly on his computer.

Knowing when I'm being dismissed, I turn to leave, bowing up and hitching the front of my body toward Puff Daddy.

The bird stands to his full height, wings spread as his head bounces up and down. "Come at me, bro!"

I shake my head as I open the office door to leave, laughing when I hear a squawked, "Pussy."

Like the bird is a human, Wren begins to argue with the thing. Luckily, I can close the door and not have to listen to them.

"New job?" Kit asks as I cross the breakroom area and head toward the coffee machine.

I narrow my eyes at him. He should be the one holding this damn list, not me.

"And why exactly couldn't you do this?" I wave the paper before placing it on the counter.

"I have other jobs coming up that conflict with the class schedule."

"How convenient," I mutter as I pop a dark roast pod into the single cup coffee machine.

"You really are irritated with this, aren't you?"

I grunt in response without turning back to face him.

"You're going to have the undivided attention of over a dozen women. What man doesn't want that?"

"Me."

He chuckles.

"This is a job better suited for Brooks," I tell him, and this isn't the first time I've mentioned it either.

"Brooks would probably end up in an orgy," my boss says as he walks right into the middle of our conversation.

"There's an orgy?" the man in question asks as he trails behind.

"See?" Kit says as he points to the most charming man we have on the team. "He'd never get any work done."

I look at Deacon as I lift the cup of black coffee to my lips, wondering if he'd consider a change for this class.

"Ignacio is a great instructor," I say, praising our language expert. "What if there's someone that speaks a different language?"

"All students in this current class speak English," Deacon says. "And Alex has baseball practice on Thursday evenings."

I can't argue with Ignacio spending time with his son. Hell, a couple months ago, he didn't even know he had a son. He's spending as much time as he can with the thirteen-year-old kid to make up for all of that lost time.

"I know you don't want to do this," Deacon continues. "And that's why you're perfect for the job."

I honestly feel like a sullen child not getting his way, but not only would throwing a tantrum not change anything, I'd never stoop so low.

"Jude is great with weapons as well," I hedge, but great is probably an overstatement.

My best friend, Jude Morris, is Blackbridge's in-house medic, science expert, and biological warfare expert. He could easily disarm a bomb, but I doubt he could hit a target from ten yards.

"If he shoots like he throws a baseball, then he's more of a hindrance than helpful," Brooks says with a wry grin.

I hold back the laugh at remembering the black eye he sported for a week last year after Jude smacked him in the face while playing ball at the park. He complained more about the bruising than I ever will about taking on this six-week class. The man is vain to the bone. Granted, the jobs he takes use his handsomeness as a weapon, but even when he's not working, he doesn't know how to turn it off.

"Jude isn't comfortable in large groups," Deacon says, making it sound like my friend is antisocial, when in fact, he really just doesn't like people. It's a completely relatable trait to have, in my opinion. "But the class isn't until tomorrow, and we have work to do today. Quinten, let's go over that case you just wrapped up."

I snatch the list of names off the counter and follow my boss back to his office, tossing a middle finger over my shoulder when the guys start to laugh.

Chapter 2

Hayden

"What are you doing?"

I don't startle at the sound of my best friend, Parker's voice when she opens my front door. I saw her pull up in the driveway, and she has a key. I also don't acknowledge her. This day has been coming for two weeks, and with each hour it drew closer, the more I hate the idea of it.

"You aren't even ready," she hisses. "We talked about this, Hayden."

I continue to use the sponge I've cut to fit in the tracks of my windows, frowning when the stupid thing just pushes the dirt to the end rather than actually cleaning it.

"Hayden," she groans. "Go get ready. We're going to be late."

"I decided I don't want to go."

"Do you realize how exclusive it is to get into this class?"

I do, actually, because she's been more excited than me to go.

The class she's referring to is a six-session course that teaches gun safety and shooting. I used to hate guns, and I'm only now considering the use of one for protection. Coming home to a kicked in door and a trashed house will make a person change their stance on a few things.

"It's for your safety," she urges. "Put the cleaning shit down and let's go."

Safe.

What a concept. I was never worried about my safety before. Like most women, I took precautions when they were needed. I don't walk alone at night. I very seldomly go to bars or clubs, and when I do it's always with a friend. I don't leave drinks unattended or meet strangers off of dating apps.

A couple of weeks ago I was safe.

Then I fell victim to a burglary. I don't know if I'll ever feel completely safe again. It doesn't matter that I changed the locks and situated my furniture where I would be alerted if someone tried to sneak in.

I still can't sleep in total darkness. I still take quick showers in place of the long, relaxing ones I used to take because I'm terrified of getting caught off guard. Hell, I've been washing my hair in the kitchen sink because I'm terrified of getting caught completely naked with soap in my eyes. I peek out of my windows each time I hear a noise, wondering if today is going to be the day they come back and take more than my damn television.

My privacy was invaded, my sanctuary violated. My skin crawls just thinking about it, and I have to drop the sponge and rub at the goosebumps forming on my arms.

"I don't think this is the right solution," I mutter as I turn to face her. I hate the look of sympathy in her eyes.

"You wanted to do this."

"You wanted me to do this," I clarify. "I simply mentioned taking a self-defense class."

I roll my eyes as I pick up the sponge and the bottle of cleaner I was using and carry them back to the kitchen.

"This is a self-defense class," she argues. "Wouldn't you rather shoot than have to grapple with some guy three times your size?"

I spin around and glare at her.

Her hands go up beside her ears. "That wasn't a jab at how small you are, but physics is a real thing, Hayden. Even a skilled hundred-pound fighter would have trouble wrestling with a two-hundred-pound man. Is that what you're wearing?"

I look down at the blouse and slacks I'm still wearing from work.

"Yeah."

"Okay, let's go. If you do well in class, I'll take you for dinner after."

Knowing I won't be able to get out of it, I grumble as I grab my purse. Parker doesn't complain once as I spend the next minute locking the two deadbolts on my front door, and she only groans once when I realize I didn't leave the front porch light on, and I have to unlock it again to turn it on.

"This is going to be a lot of fun," Parker says with a wide grin as we drive to the gun range. "I showed you the pictures online, right?"

"More than once," I mutter as I watch the city rush by through the passenger window.

"These guys are so hot. The guy teaching the class has a beard and tattoos. He's so sexy."

I would feel like she's more interested in flirting during class than supporting me, but I know that she's worried about me. I haven't taken the burglary well at all.

"Just type in hashtag Blackbridge Special on your phone and you can see for yourself," she urges.

I oblige her because it's easier than arguing. I turn the phone to face her. "This guy?"

"Hot, right?"

"This guy is your type, not mine."

"That would mean something if you had a type."

I ignore the jab.

"Look at the other guys. All of their pictures are on their website, but I'm calling dibs on the instructor."

"Dibs?" I mutter as I swipe through the images on the phone. I'd never tell her, but all the guys are good looking in their own way. The images are like a damned photo gallery for hot models rather than a security firm. It makes me wonder if clients let them slide with half-assed work just because they're handsome. "Dibs is for kids fighting over a game system controller, not for claiming a man you've never met before."

"Are you saying you want dibs on the instructor?"

I look up at her. "What? No. I'm not interested in any of them."

Plus, the guy showcased on the website as tonight's instructor is massive. Yeah, he's got sexy tattoos and a glorious beard, but he also looks to be more than twice my size. He looks dangerous and angry, and that doesn't appeal to me one bit.

Parker is wrong about not having a type. I do have a type, sort of. Although my dating life has been limited, more so in the last couple of years, I've always ended up in relationships with clean-cut professionals. Other than the short-lived crush I had on David Beckham years ago, rugged, tattooed men never really turned my head. This guy, Quinten Lake, looks like someone I would run from, not flirt with.

"Do you have everything you need?" Parker asks, making me realize I was staring at his picture on my phone for longer than I'd like to admit.

"Need? What the hell do I need? You set this up, not me."

"Just your driver's license. Calm down. This is supposed to be empowering, not a punishment."

I take a deep breath as I climb out of her car. Nerves make my fingers tremble as I wait for her at the front of the car. Maybe the graphic designer on the website photoshopped him to look meaner than he actually is. I mean, wouldn't it draw in more customers if the guy teaching the class looked like a serious badass?

The guy at the front counter of the business looks nothing like the man on the website, I observe as Parker signs us in.

"Just through there, ladies," the clerk says, pointing to a door off to the side.

Several pairs of expectant eyes look up at us when we enter, and with the way they handled the marketing on their website, I'm not surprised to find nothing but women in the room. The surly guy is missing as we take our seats and wait for the class to start.

I'm calming down, feeling a little more comfortable that we're in a classroom setting rather than in a concrete room with guns lying all around.

Parker, being the social person that she is, starts a conversation with the woman on her right, and before long they're both snickering about how hot these guys are. All conversation comes to a halt when the door opens and a man walks in.

If anything, the graphic designer played down this guy's size. He's massive, his build beyond imposing. His jet-black hair is cut short, but still somehow styled nicely. His dark beard is nearly long enough to brush his t-shirt as he walks up to the front of the classroom while looking down at a piece of paper in his hands.

When he looks up scanning the room, the contrast of his bright blue eyes makes me feel exposed. I clear my throat, straightening in my seat as his face turns in our direction.

"Welcome," he grunts to his captive audience. "We're going to start with roll call, then we have some paperwork to get out of the way before we get started on the class."

His voice is rough and gravelly, but instead of it making me feel uncomfortable, I find myself a little entranced as he calls out the names on the list.

"Hayden," Parker says with a nudge to my side.

"Hayden Prescott?" he says, and I can tell by his tone that it isn't the first time he's read my name from his list.

"Present!" I snap, raising my hand with awkwardness.

He frowns in my direction before moving his gaze slightly to my right to focus on Parker.

Why all of a sudden do I feel like I should shove her out of her chair and kick her under the table?

"And who are you?" the man all but growls.

Parker preens a little, a vibrant smile spreading across her face. "I'm Parker Maxwell. I'm Hayden's best friend. It's nice to meet y—"

"You're not on my list," he interrupts.

"I signed in at the front." Parker's smile doesn't fade.

"If you're not on the list, you can't join the class. Did you get an email confirmation?"

"I didn't personally sign up for the class. I'm here with Hayden."

"This class is only for confirmed attendees." He keeps his eyes locked on her, both of them not speaking until it becomes so awkward that the other women in the room begin to shift uncomfortably in their seats. "You need to leave so we can get started."

Now that pretty, practiced smile slides off my friend's face.

"Let's just go," I mutter as I begin to stand from my seat.

"You don't have to leave, Ms. Prescott," the man says.

"I'm not staying if she can't stay."

He doesn't say another word as we both stand and make our way out of the room.

I didn't want to be here in the first place, but I'd be lying if I said I wasn't upset to be called out like we were.

"We can just sign up together for the next class," Parker says as she loops her arm through mine as we leave the building. "Let's go grab dinner."

That's Parker for you—quick to make new plans when others fall through.

"I'm not going to a bar to eat dinner," I say as we make our way across the parking lot.

Hairs on the back of my neck stand up, but I blame the setting sun and the cool evening breeze.

"It's called a pub, not a bar."

"And I'd prefer a restaurant that's not crowded."

She huffs but quickly agrees. She knows I can just as easily go home and cook and be happier than going out and being around other people.

"Fine," she says. "But I want sushi."

Chapter 3

Quinten

"You can suck it!"

"I'm not arguing with you about this," Wren grumbles as I walk into his office.

"Stupid fucking cat!" Puff Daddy screeches.

I'd say he's in rare form, throwing a fit while pacing back and forth along one of his perches, but this is just classic behavior for the verbally aggressive bird.

"What's the problem now?" I ask, not one hundred percent sure I even want to know.

"He's still pissed about the cat," Wren mutters, his attention still mostly on the information he's compiling on his computer.

"You left me here last night!" Puff wails before making a realistic crying noise.

"Because you said you didn't want to go home," Wren argues, his voice flat yet irritated.

"The Hilton has free breakfast!"

I laugh at the stupid bird.

"And I have a perfectly good condo. I'm not staying in a hotel because you can't get along with your brother."

"Stepbrother!" the bird corrects. "He's Satan's best friend!"

"So fucking glad I live alone," I mutter as I plop down the stack of papers in front of him.

"He's fine with Whitney, but he hates the cat."

"Look at my ass!" The bird turns around, waving his little feathery butt in our direction. "It's flat. Chicks love a full ass."

"Those grow back?" I ask, pointing to the lack of red tail feathers.

"Takes six to eight weeks," Wren explains. "He's just impatient."

"I've been violated!"

"And why doesn't he just stay away from the fucking cat?"

Wren turns to face me, a wide grin on his face. "That cat is surprisingly agile, and his ability to climb the curtains is uncanny. There are only thirteen here. You're missing one."

Wren taps the edge of the paperwork I just handed him on his desk to straighten it.

"One woman showed up with a friend."

"So, there should be fifteen," he says in a tone that tells me he's making fun of my math skills.

"They left." He frowns. "I told the friend she wasn't registered, so she had to leave. The other woman left, too."

I don't go into detail that it's probably a good thing because that friend had a glint in her eye that only spelled trouble. She was there for the very reason so many other women completed the form. I'm still in a position to blame that stupid trending hashtag for this entire mess. Which also reminds me to smack Flynn in the back of the head the next time I see him for ending up on the front cover of those stupid gossip magazines with his woman.

Wren shuffles through the paperwork once again. "Hayden Prescott?"

"I guess," I tell him with a shrug, but it's fake indifference.

I spent a little too long last night watching her stand from the table, gather her things, and walk out of the room. I knew why she was there, and it had everything to do with her size and nothing to do with knowing any detail about what's going on in her life to have been flagged by Wren's online bots leading to her selection for the class.

She's fucking tiny, a little wisp of a woman who probably wouldn't even come up to the bottom of my beard if she were standing on her tiptoes. Hell, she's so slight an attacker would probably still laugh at her if she were pointing a gun in his face. If I saw her from behind, I'd mistake her for a child.

But I didn't see her from behind. I got a full front view of the woman, and there's nothing childlike about her. Not the curve of her breasts in that silky blouse she was wearing. Not the deep penetrating gaze she seemed reluctant to throw my way.

No. Hayden Prescott is all woman, just in a miniature package.

It's another reason why I'm so floored that she garnered so much of my attention last night.

I like my women sturdy. I don't want to end up hurting one of them on accident when I—

Shit, why am I even letting my head go there right now? I'll never see her again.

"You have to call her and get her back in the class."

"Uh, what?" If I had a little bubble above my head, this man would've just popped the damn thing.

"Hayden Prescott needs to be in that class. Were you not listening when I explained that every one of those women were handpicked for a reason?"

"Is she one of the ones with domestic abuse in her background?" I ask, breaking the rule I set for myself not to get too invested in any of their stories.

It's not because I don't care, but it's hard to fight the urge to fix things when I find them broken, and nothing fixes a man who hurts women than his own trip to the emergency room.

"She had a home burglary."

"People get robbed all the time. Does she live in a shitty neighborhood?"

"Her address is in a nicer part of town, but she lives alone. She doesn't have many friends."

"She had a friend last night," I mumble, still able to picture the glint in her friend's eyes as she tried to smile her way into the class.

"What's her friend's name?" Wren asks as he turns back to his computer.

"Parker something or other."

"Parker Maxwell?"

"Sounds right."

"She's not flagged at all for needing the class."

"And I could tell that about her last night."

That's not completely true. Many women are well-versed at being able to hide what's going on in their personal lives, but that woman is a man-eater through and through. I've dealt with my share of them in the past, mostly for clients who have interacted with them and were left with the short end of the stick.

"Looks like you're going to have fifteen in the class."

"They left. Put them both in the next class." I make a mental note to suddenly be busy if Deacon decides to host another one of these training classes.

"She needs help now. Just give her a call and tell her that she can come to the next class with her friend."

I close my eyes and take a long, frustrated breath in through my nose. "Sure thing."

"And Quinten?" Wren says before I can leave his office. "It would be best if I could get that paperwork to Pam by the weekend."

"It's Friday," I remind him.

He just grins before turning back around to finish working on whatever he was doing before I interrupted.

He's back to arguing with the damned bird before I can close the door.

I spend five minutes chatting with Jude in the breakroom before heading to my office. What I did yesterday wasn't a mistake, but there's no way to call someone and tell them to come back after making them leave without sounding like an asshole.

As I sit in my office chair, I wonder if I could get Pam to call Hayden and get her up here to sign the stupid paperwork. After ten minutes of staring at the phone, I look up her information in our computer system and make the call.

"Hello?" she says, answering after the third ring.

So much for just leaving a voicemail.

"Hayden Prescott?"

"I'm not interested."

"Excuse me?" I ask, confused.

"I don't care about an extended warranty. My roof is fine, and vinyl siding would look terrible on my house."

I fight a laugh, wondering how many calls she gets for those types of things that she went through the whole spiel that quickly. I guess I'm just lucky she isn't screening her calls, or unlucky depending on how you look at it.

"This is Quinten Lake with Blackbridge Security. I'm—"

"The giant jerk."

I pause, not sure if she's using *giant* in reference to my size or level of jerkiness.

"I'm the instructor for the shooting safety class."

"Look, I didn't want to go to that stupid class to begin with. I had no idea that Parker wasn't registered. I don't understand a follow-up call after being embarrassed. It's not like I'm planning on leaving a bad *Yelp* review or something, so you're wasting both of our time."

This woman is so fucking feisty, and I must be crazy because I kind of like it. She's like a stack of short-fused dynamite in a tiny little package.

"I've been told by my office manager that there was a mix up. You and your friend are welcome to rejoin the class." I shake my head, knowing that sounded like a personal apology rather than some type of processing mistake. "I'll just need you to swing by our main office at some point today to complete the paperwork."

Silence fills the line, but the timer on the phone display is still clicking off the seconds, so I know she hasn't hung up.

"Let me get this straight, you kick us out of class, realize it's a mistake, and then expect me to spend my time coming to you to complete paperwork I could've easily done last night?"

I open my mouth to argue that I didn't ask her to leave, that it was her friend who was the unauthorized attendee, but there's no sense in arguing the point.

"It'll only take a few minutes," I say instead.

"The drive wouldn't. Can I not just complete the paperwork at the next class?"

"We'll need to go over the information you missed at last night's class." I find myself wanting to rile her up just to get another taste of her hair-trigger attitude. "I'll need to reschedule that class for you sometime during the week. What day—"

"I can give you an hour before the next class, and that's it."

The corner of my mouth turns up. "Are you a fast learner?"

"I'm not an idiot, if that's what you're asking. What does the first class entail?"

"Missouri laws regarding handguns," I answer.

"So nothing that requires actually touching them?"

"Correct."

"I'll bring a notepad an hour early."

"I have a pamphlet. So, you don't—"

The call goes dead, and I find myself equally entertained and annoyed as I place the handset back on the receiver.

She's like a chihuahua. The size of a small animal with the attitude of a fierce lion.

Finding myself restless, I head back to the breakroom for a bottle of water.

"I hear you kicked someone out of your class last night," Jude says as I enter the room.

Deacon's head swirls around, his focus on the sandwich he's making gone. "What?"

I glare at my friend for throwing me under the bus.

"Of course, you heard already. I would question Wren's dedication to gossip if he let an hour go by without relaying our conversation word for word." I make my way to the fridge, opting for an energy drink instead of water. "One of the women showed up with a friend that wasn't registered."

"You should've let her stay," Deacon says before bringing his food to his mouth and biting into it.

"She left with her friend, but before you complain, I just got off the phone with her and let her know that her friend was more than welcome to come to class. We've made arrangements for her to come early to cover the material she missed last night."

Satisfied with my explanation, Deacon nods before leaving to head back to his office.

I kick Jude's foot when our boss's office door closes.

"Dick," I mutter.

He grins widely. He knows that we aren't micromanaged by Deacon like some people are by their bosses, but I still don't like having to explain myself. If I'm going to be given autonomy to work, then I don't need those decisions being analyzed.

"Just for that, I think you need to come help during one class."

He doesn't answer, instead pulling a length of rope from his pocket as he begins to tie it in different sized knots.

Chapter 4

Hayden

"He's full of shit," I grumble, my foot tapping on the linoleum floor with my arms crossed over my chest.

"Maybe one person in the office told him one thing and someone else told him something different. It happens at your job all the time," Parker says.

"And that explains the reason for making us leave last week, but then to have the audacity to expect me to drive across town to sign some paperwork? Geez, doesn't the man know how to scan documents into email?"

I shouldn't be taking my irritation out on Parker, but even though I argued about what time I'd be here tonight when Quinten called last Friday, I had no real intention of showing up. If I hadn't been so fired up that I called Parker to complain about the jerk, I could be sitting at home in my pajamas watching baking show reruns.

She all but squealed when I told her we could go back, and here we are… waiting because although Quinten was adamant about needing to go over this information, he's the one who's late.

"Would you quit?" Parker hisses when I turn my arm to look at my watch again.

"He's late. It's rude."

"It's two minutes past. Maybe he got caught in traffic or had a—" The door to the classroom opens, cutting off her words. "There he is. Hi, Mr. Lake."

"Quinten," he grunts. "Sorry I'm late."

He doesn't offer an excuse, and I know I'm just being petty over two minutes, but that annoys me too. Not that I should be concerned about where he's been. Only a crazy woman would wonder what a man she doesn't even know has been up to, and I'm anything but crazy.

"Sign these." He pulls two sheets of paper with fine print on them and places them in front of each of us.

Parker uses the ink pen on the table to scribble her name at the bottom.

"You need to read that," I hiss.

She shrugs as I turn my attention back to the form, reading it word for word, slower than it would normally take me because if he's going to waste my time, then I'm petty enough to waste a little of his.

Only when I finish reading about liability and instructional rules, do I look up at him. I find a small smile playing at the corners of his mouth instead of a frown of irritation. I can't tell if he's happy I've taken the time to read it, or if it's an agreement to my pettiness that he's accepting as a challenge.

I scrawl my name before sliding the paper back across the table to him.

"I was trying to explain these when you hung up on me last week," he says as he hands each of us a rather drab looking informational pamphlet.

"You hung up on him?" Parker hisses as if the man isn't standing just a few feet away.

I shrug, refusing to apologize. "I thought the conversation was over."

"As you can see…"

He spends the next twenty minutes going over the pamphlet word for word, as if neither one of us can read. Parker seems a little too happy to listen to him talk, and personally, I find myself listening to the tone and cadence of his voice rather than the actual words.

He's in the front of the class, acting as if neither of us exist by the time the other women start piling in through the door.

Several in the group look in our direction, appearing unhappy that we're back, but I'm used to that sort of thing when I'm with Parker. She's got the looks and the confidence that draw men in by the hundreds. Less confident women take issue with that, and it makes it difficult to make friends.

The woman she spoke with so easily last week ends up sitting a little closer to the front this week. As I look around the room, I see all the spots up front filled, whereas last week there were gaps between some of them.

We're in the back, a location of my choosing because although I would normally sit up front in an educational setting, I needed to be as far away from that man as possible. I know I should take the class seriously, and I will as far as the safety aspect is concerned, but I don't honestly see myself ever buying or carrying a firearm.

I don't think I have it in me to actually pull the trigger, even if someone is threatening me.

"Jesus," Parker mutters when he turns his back to the class and begins a crude drawing of a handgun. "Do you see how big his hands are? I bet he could palm my entire ass in just one of those things."

"Shh," one of the women sitting at the table in front of us hisses.

Parker cocks an eyebrow, but she snaps her mouth closed.

I don't answer that I have in fact noticed how big his hands are because the woman shushed us, but because I have no clue why I've even noticed something like that in a man before.

Plus, his flexing forearms and big hands don't discount his surly attitude.

All the good traits, including those pretty blue eyes lined with lashes women all over would be jealous of, don't matter if he's going to open his mouth and say something rude. Even one of those growly grunts I've heard from him more than once is too much, too irritating.

Now, if he could just stand there, maybe slowly turning in a circle every so often without making a sound, then I might consider getting excited like my best friend.

The women in the group, my best friend included, are enthralled as he draws arrows to each part on his drawing and explains what they're called and their purpose.

"And what's that near the tip?" Parker asks in a sweet voice.

He looks from her back to the board before using the side of his fist to erase it. "That's just a smudge."

Several of the women snicker, and I roll my eyes. Parker has a quality check she does on men, and Quinten not playing into her ditzy woman trap by wasting time explaining why a smudge was on the board like he's talking to a child just rocketed him up a little further on her scale.

I swear if he calls someone ma'am or holds a door open, I'll never hear the end of it from her.

***

"You're going to need to find a handgun that feels comfortable in your hand. Grip is very important," he explains thirty minutes later. "I want you to move around to the different stations to see which one feels the most comfortable. If none of them do, let me know and we can find something that does."

We've moved to the actual gun range part of the building. It's a long, narrow room sectioned off to make seven lanes.

"Not on the trigger," he says loud enough for everyone to hear through the earmuffs we're all required to wear in this room.

I push the flimsy glasses back up on my nose, knowing I look just as silly as everyone else in the room wearing these stupid things, but still feeling singled out each time he looks in my direction. Of course, he has on super cool looking glasses and sleek black earmuffs, whereas we're all wearing either bright orange or bright green ones, looking like we're getting ready to go into the woods to hunt for food.

I scowl at Parker when she tries to hand me the gun.

"Place it down on the table in front of you. Do not hand over a gun to someone else. Do not move a firearm from one lane to another. When we're in here, I will do that for you. When at the gun range, the range officer will do that."

Obediently, Parker lays the black gun down on the little table at the head of the lane we've been assigned, and I just look down at the thing. Never in my life have I held a gun. Not a real one anyway, and I don't think this is going to have the same feel of the Nerf power blaster I used once at a party in college.

"So hot," Parker mutters. "Look at his forearms. Damn, I could just take a bite out of that man."

Chapter 5

Quinten

"Here," I tell Rachel. "Now you try it."

I place the Springfield XD back on the table at the head of the lane and take a step back.

"Good, now position your hands like this." I show her with my empty hands how to stack them around the grip.

"Like this?" She moves her fingers, but they're still in the wrong position.

"Like this." I turn to the side so she can see my hands better. I'm not going to touch her, and I don't get the vibe that she even wants that.

"Like those jeans should be illegal. Do you see his ass, Hayden? That man does squats."

"Both thumbs pointing forward like this," I say while trying to ignore Parker Maxwell.

There are two things most newbies in a gun range don't realize. One being they talk several levels louder because their own hearing is muffled. Two, any person that knows their way around a weapon is going to wear a pair of electronic compression earmuffs. That means I can hear what everyone around the room is saying even though they can't hear each other unless they speak louder. Hayden's friend Parker is practically yelling at this point.

"Better," I tell Rachel. "This seems a little big. Is it comfortable? Nope, finger off the trigger."

"Maybe something a little smaller?" She scrunches her nose as she places the weapon back down on the carpet-covered table.

"There's a Ruger at lane four that may be a better fit. Go try it out."

I step back even further as she heads in that direction.

The women are excited. Some are apprehensive, never having touched a gun before and some are anxious to load up and send some shit down the lane. One woman, Gayle, I'm going to have to ask Wren about because she seems like she's ready to take someone down at the knees, and there may also be a little hint of vigilante justice in her eyes.

"Strong thighs. I bet that man could go for hours without tiring. His feet. Geez, what are they like, a size thirteen?"

Fifteen, but who honestly cares?

I could tell Parker that I can hear every word she's saying, but where's the fun in that?

"How are we doing over here?" I ask as I approach the pair.

Parker is busy ogling me, and Hayden is frowning down at the Glock 43/42 like it's personally set out to ruin her week.

"How does it feel in your hand?" I ask when she doesn't answer.

"She hasn't picked it up yet," Parker explains, her eyes trailing up and down my body unabashedly.

I focus all of my attention on Hayden. "Are you afraid of it?"

"No," she answers swiftly.

"Next week we're going to be shooting, so you'll need to know which one is most comfortable." I pick it up and hold it in my hands. I could never use a gun this small. "Hold it like this."

I demonstrate the proper hold even though my hand is much too big to do it the right way.

"Now you try."

I place it back on the table and take a step back.

"Excuse me," I mutter when I bump into Parker.

"My pleasure. I mean sorry." Parker bites the corner of her lip, and I'm sure any man looking for her kind of trouble would find it appealing, but it doesn't faze me.

"Go ahead."

Hayden mutters something about watching TV as she reaches for the Glock.

"Like this," I say when she finally has it in her hands. I lift my hands and show her the proper grip just like I did for Rachel a few minutes ago.

"It's heavier than I thought it would be," she says before putting it back down.

"It's less than a pound and a half, but it will weigh a little more when it's loaded. Maybe the Sig Sauer P238 would be better? There's one down in lane six. Go check it out." I step out of the way as Parker drags Hayden to the other end of the room, keeping an eye on her as she approaches lane six. She's still not enthusiastic, but she picks it up, turning it from side to side rather than just glaring at the thing like it personally offended her like she did in lane one when I first approached her.

"What size bullets does this one take?" one of the other women asks.

"Caliber," I correct. "This one and the Glock in lane one use 9mm rounds."

"I want something with a lot of power," Gayle says from lane three.

I head over and explain the difference in ammunition to Gayle but keep my eye on Hayden. It's clear she doesn't want to be here. It's also evident that her friend is beginning to frustrate her with all of her sexualized comments about me. At the same time, I can tell she doesn't care that I'm even around.

I don't notice Hayden throwing sly glances my way or looking at me from under her eyelashes. She seems to have a chip on her shoulder about something, and it makes me wonder if there's more going on in her life than a house break-in. Don't get me wrong, that's a serious violation of someone's life, but she doesn't seem too enthusiastic about taking back that power and control of her safety.

I regret not looking into her more and reading her entire file, but then I have to remind myself that I'm here to teach a class, not to situate myself into her life beyond these concrete walls.

"You're not Dirty Harry," I tell Gayle when she mimics a fast draw from the table, making popping noise with her mouth. "Finger off the trigger unless you plan to shoot. If you do that while it is loaded, then you're sure to hurt yourself or someone else."

"No fun," she grumbles, but she sets the gun back down.

Once everyone has made their way around the room and have all nodded—except for Hayden, of course—when I asked if they found the one they want to start with, I guide them back to the classroom.

"Next week we're going to start practicing on loading and unloading as well as a short session on shooting," I begin. "I don't want anyone to go out and buy a gun until after you've shot more than one. You won't know what you're most comfortable with until you fire a couple of them. Targets as well as the ammunition is provided, so you don't have to worry about bringing anything extra to class."

There's an air of excitement spreading through the room as I continue to discuss the plans for next week, but Hayden has her eyes focused on her fingers, messing with her cuticles as I speak. If Wren and Deacon could see how unmotivated she is to learn and interact, maybe they wouldn't have made such a big deal about her being in this class.

"Any questions?"

Eyes dart all around the room as the women wait for someone else to speak up. I hate that some of them have gone through things in their lives that make them uncomfortable to ask a question.

"Anything?"

"Will we have gun powder on us when we leave?" Gayle asks.

"You will have lead particles on you, but there's D-Lead soap in the bathroom to wash your hands after we're done. Any other questions?"

"What about our clothes?" Gayle asks.

Hayden looks toward her, forehead scrunched between her eyes.

"Yes, particles will be on your clothing. Just wash as normal."

"But like, what if we get stopped by the cops and they test our arms and clothing?"

I tilt my head to the side, knowing I need to speak with Wren sooner rather than later about this woman.

"I'm not following. Police don't just randomly test you during a routine traffic stop."

Too many women in this group are blinking up at me as if they have the same questions in their own head, and it makes me reconsider the benefit of this group. Are we training them to defend themselves or hurt someone who hurt them?

"What if I'm questioned?" Gayle continues. "You guys keep a log of when I'm here and for how long, right?"

"Yes, but—"

"Ladies," Parker says with a humor-filled tone. "It ruins your alibi if you have to ask for an alibi."

Hayden rolls her lips between her teeth, and I know she's trying not to smile. Her eyes sparkle and damn if it isn't a good look on her. Does it make me a misogynist asshole to think that she should do it more often? I guess I actually want her to find more reasons in her life to smile.

"Any other questions?" They shake their heads. "See you ladies next week."

They all move to stand as I gather my things from the table at the front of the room.

"Hayden can you hold back?"

Her friend smiles whereas Hayden has lost the glow of happiness she had a moment ago. I can admit she's even pretty when she frowns.

"I can see if they have a Walther PPK if you want to test the grip before you leave."

"The last one I had was good," she says.

"Are you sure?"

"Yeah. Anything else?"

"No," I answer.

"We're going out for drinks," Parker interjects. "Would you like to join us?"

I don't miss the slight shake of Hayden's head, but even if I were in the mood to get her riled up, I wouldn't accept the offer. I have plans with Jude tonight that include a six-pack of beer and a hockey game on television. Being around fifteen women for the last two hours has managed to drain me.

"I have plans," I tell her. "But maybe another time."

"Sure thing," Parker says, running her hand down my arm in a friendly gesture. Suddenly, I realize I was wrong about Hayden and her lack of attention in my direction because her eyes flare a little at the sight of her friend's hand on my arm.

"You ladies be safe," I say as I step away from the touch.

Parker assures me they will be, and Hayden just turns around and walks out of the classroom without saying a word.

Chapter 6

Hayden

"Wanna join us for drinks?" I mimic sarcastically in a high-pitched voice that sounds nothing like the one Parker used just a few minutes ago when we were standing in front of that man.

"Are you jealous? If you want to flirt with him, I'll step back, but the man is fine. If you don't go after him, then I'm going to," she warns.

"He's not a painting at an auction, Parker. Maybe the man isn't interested in either of us."

"That's not a *no* or a *go ahead and take your shot, Parker*," she says with a wide smile. I get the feeling she's up to something, and I'm idiotically playing right into the middle of whatever it is.

"Do we have to go for drinks? We could just grab a bottle of wine and hang out at your apartment for a while," I say, changing the subject as quickly as I can. It won't distract her for long, but it will divert her attention long enough that I can think of how I want to respond.

I hate wine, but I hate the idea of going home alone again even worse. I never thought my quaint little house would give me the creeps, but it hasn't felt like home since the night it was broken into. I shudder at the realization of what could've happened to me had I not stayed late at work that evening.

"Drinks," Parker insists. "You need to live a little. You'll never find a man if you stay holed up at home all the time."

"I'm not looking for a man," I remind her. "And I suggested your place not mine. That's a change of scenery for me. I have no interest in a bar."

And it's true. She always comes to my place because before the break-in, I never wanted to leave. I was comfortable in my space. I hate that someone took that from me.

"You're going to have to get over your fear of being around people."

"I'm not afraid to be around people. You make me sound agoraphobic. I don't like loud places, especially ones where people are drinking and acting like idiots."

"You've been going to the wrong places."

"I've been going to the places you drag me to," I remind her.

She gives me a quick smile and a simple shake of her head as if I'm acting ridiculous. I know there are lots of people like me in the world. Not wanting to be in a crowd or having to yell over loud music isn't a concept I created.

"I read reviews online about this little place down the street. You may find that you like it. Come on."

Begrudgingly, I follow her to the car. The gun range is somewhat isolated on the edge of town, so walking isn't an option. It probably wouldn't be safe either.

"Oh, look!" Parker beams with her finger pointing to the front of the bar as we get out of the car. "It's half-priced drinks for ladies' night, so that means mostly women."

Maybe she thinks I'm an idiot, but I'm well aware that ladies' night means the men come out in full force in hopes of flirting with the women trying to get a discounted drink. We've been down this road before.

I don't want to ruin her fun, so I plaster the best fake smile I can manage and follow her inside.

The place is small, and thankfully the music isn't playing very loudly. I'd say the ratio of men to women is about equal, and although most people are talking and having a good time in small groups, several heads turn in our direction when we step over the threshold.

This is another thing I'm used to. Parker turns heads with her tall, svelte frame, long blond hair, and pouty lips, and if she doesn't catch someone's attention with all of that, they're a goner once they look into her stormy-gray eyes.

"I like this place already," she says with a wide smile as we cross the room and head to the bar. "Do you want a beer?"

I tilt my head and roll me eyes.

"Two martinis," she tells the bartender, ordering our preferred drinks before turning back to look at me. "I'm only having one, but feel free to cut loose."

"I have work tomorrow."

We wait patiently for our drink order, Parker turning around to scope out the people around us while I just focus on her. I don't need to make eye contact with anyone because it could lead to an awkward conversation. I struggle with my brain-to-mouth filter when I'm in a situation I'm not enjoying, and I'm quick to say something to get myself out of it.

The last time we ended up at a place like this and a guy approached me while Parker was in the restroom, he introduced himself and my response was, "Umm, no."

It came across as extremely rude, and although I wanted to be left alone, I wasn't intentionally meaning to sound like a complete stuck-up bitch. From the four-letter words he tossed my way before moving on to the next woman sitting alone, that's exactly how he saw me.

"They should have a ladies' only night," I tell her as the bartender slides us our drinks.

"They do at The Cherry Stem." Parker lifts her drink to her mouth, winking at me over the rim.

"That's a gay bar."

"Exactly."

"My point is these places would appeal to me more if I could come in and have a drink without being bothered."

She gives me a rueful smile. "Keep that look on your face and you won't have to worry about it. That snarl screams unapproachable."

"Maybe I should hang out with ugly friends, and then I wouldn't have to worry about the look on my face."

She scoffs. "Are you trying to imply that you're ugly, too? Because I don't have ugly friends. Let's find a table."

I point to an empty one in the corner but leave it to Parker to lead us to one that's more centered in the room.

"Besides," Parker continues as we pull stools away from the pub-style table. "Being approached has more to do with type and attitude than looks."

"Then that ruins your unapproachable remark. I'm always sending off don't-approach-me vibes when we go out."

"Exactly, and some men find that as a challenge. Add in the fact that you're pint-sized, and it turns a lot of men on. They see you as feisty. Women sitting alone and minding their own business are looked at as shy, and it makes men wonder what they're like in bed. Men have specific tastes when they're dating."

"People don't go to bars to date, Parker. They're looking for people to hook up with."

She shrugs her shoulders as if the two mean the same thing.

"Enough about men."

I snap my head back. Parker always wants to talk about men. My eyes narrow as she takes another sip from her drink.

"You need to lay everything out on the table. I'm not a psychologist, but I'm here to listen."

"About what?" I ask, hating that there isn't a napkin on the table for me to shred so I have something to do with my hands.

"You've been a little different since the break-in."

"Wouldn't you be if you came home to your door kicked in and all of your belongings rifled through?"

"I would," she agrees.

"I had to buy brand-new underwear and bras because I couldn't stomach the idea of putting something so close to my body that some strange criminal touched."

Her look softens. "Oh, babe. I'm sorry. Are you still having trouble sleeping?"

"Yes," I confess. "Every third night or so I'm exhausted enough from not sleeping well the two nights before that I sleep hard, but then the cycle continues."

"I know you changed the locks."

I nod, but honestly, I had locks before. The door was smashed— another thing I had to replace—not opened with a key, so the locks don't provide as much of a sense of security as I thought they would when I purchased them.

"What else have you done?"

"I've called about getting a security system, but they have a waitlist. The last place I called said it would be weeks before they got to me, but then I also think about the horror stories of people getting broken into by the people who set up their systems, and it makes me wonder if that's any safer or just making me more of a target."

"Have you considered ordering online and doing it yourself?"

I huff a humorless laugh. "Do you remember I needed hands-on help when I managed to change the language on my phone to German? I could never do something like that myself. Would you happen to know anyone you'd trust to do it?"

She gives me a wry smile. "I don't exactly stay in contact with the men I date when it's over."

"Well, keep me in mind next time you're on the prowl. Maybe you can land someone with extreme technical skills that would be willing to help a friend."

"Are you pimping me out for a home security system?"

I grin, knowing she's not really offended. "Whatever it takes."

I take another sip of my drink, thinking that tonight didn't turn out so bad after all.

"Okay, enough about the sad stuff. Do you think the rumors about hand size are true where Quinten is concerned?"

Chapter 7

Quinten

"I'm telling you, she's going to end up killing someone."

Wren just grins from his stance near the coffee pot.

"Who?" Jude asks from his favorite spot on the sofa.

"This woman in the gun class," I explain.

"No, I know that part. Who is she going to kill?"

"I don't have a clue, but she's a little too excited about shooting, and the questions about gun powder residue and getting questioned by the police, it's like she's looking for an alibi."

"She sounds fierce," Wren says with a wide smile. "Which woman is it?"

"Gayle. What did she flag for?"

Wren tilts his head as he shuffles through the gobs of information in his brain. "If my memory is serving me correctly, Gayle has had a series of abusive relationships. The last one is in prison and isn't scheduled for release anytime soon. So, she should be okay."

"Well, the woman is definitely ready to take her power back. I'm just afraid she's going to enforce that power through the business end of a Glock."

"Would it be so bad?" Wren asks, his face once again serious.

"Her killing someone?"

"Killing an abuser," Jude clarifies, making me wonder if both of them have lost their minds.

"Look, I'm just as disgusted as you two are about men who hurt women, so don't misread me, but if Blackbridge is the one providing the training, I'm sure there could be repercussions for the company if one of the women goes vigilante on someone who hurt them." With the way the women were paying rapt attention to Gayle's questions, there honestly may be more than one lady in the class that has had such thoughts. "Maybe these classes were a bad idea."

"If the classes help one woman better defend herself and feel safer, then the classes are worth it," Wren says as he pushes himself away from the counter. "And the release paperwork they signed clears us of any and all legal repercussions for how they use their new skills from class."

"So you're saying you aren't going to pull Gayle from the class?" I mutter.

"Who's the issue now?" Deacon says as he joins us in the breakroom. He yawns, rubbing his eyes with the back of his hand.

"There's a woman in the class that's probably going to end up hurting someone," I explain. "Wren says not to remove her."

"Leave her alone. We aren't responsible for what others do. She has her own choices to make."

"Really?" I thought at least the boss would have a different opinion than Wren and Jude. "She could hurt people."

"Hurt people or hurt someone who hurt her?"

"Wow," I mutter. "Okay. I'll let her stay."

"If you think she's going to go on a rampage in public, then that's a different story. We can pull her and report her to the police. Do you think that?"

"No," I answer honestly.

Gayle doesn't seem like the type of person to hurt innocent people, but I also don't know who she considers worthy of a bullet either.

"There are four types of people I hate most in the world. People who hurt women, people who hurt kids, people who hurt animals, and people who don't give a courtesy flush when shitting in a public restroom." Deacon counts them off on his fingers. "As far as I'm concerned, the world is a better place without them."

"I can agree with most of that," I tell him.

"Just keep an eye on her. Wren, what's her medical situation?"

"She's been hospitalized more than once for injuries. She's in therapy and has been attending religiously for the last six months. The bots I set up were very specific to only women who were currently out of bad situations and were seeking help, because—"

"Statistically, women still in abusive situations are more likely to be abused even more if their abusers knew they were planning to leave or defend themselves," I finish.

"We're doing this to help, not hurt," Deacon adds.

"I've added hotline information on the website for those that are looking to get out. I only chose the ones that are most reputable, and I even contacted them directly to let them know what we're doing so they can refer those they think would benefit from the classes," Wren continues. "I just wish there was more that we could do."

All of us turn contemplative. When Flynn Coleman, our forensics expert who is also a former FBI agent, walks into the room, he takes a look around in confusion but doesn't say a word. We deal with a lot of heavy stuff, so it's not unusual to find a group of us in a weird mood.

"I'll talk with Anna. She has a ton of contacts in the fundraising world. Maybe we can set up a gala or something."

We all stare open-mouthed at Deacon.

"Who are you and what happened to our boss?" Jude asks.

"A gala? Do you even hear yourself?" I say.

"I bet you'd look great in a tux," Wren says.

"And we all know you do," Jude says referring to the time Deacon made Wren step in for him and go to a black-tie event.

"Not me," Wren says holding his hands up in surrender. "Don't get me wrong, I had fun that night. Dancing with a gorgeous woman and—"

Deacon growls at Wren's reference to his wife.

"Really?" Wren asks. "That's what you're getting upset about? I danced with her in public. Didn't Flynn snuggle with her on the sofa in a private hotel suite?"

"For fuck's sake," Flynn says as he takes a seat on the same sofa as Jude. "We were watching TV. She had her head in my lap."

"Yeah," Wren snaps. "Close to your—"

"We don't talk about that!" Deacon snaps, but there's no real animosity toward Flynn. The man is his best friend and in a committed relationship. That thought reminds me that I owe him a smack against the head, but now doesn't seem like the best time.

"Fine," Wren mutters, but there's still a sly smile playing on his lips. "Any other women you're worried about, Quinten."

I narrow my eyes at him. This motherfucker is always stirring the damn pot.

"Not really."

"Not even Hayden?"

"What's going on?" Deacon asks.

"Absolutely nothing," I respond a little too quickly, sounding guilty when I've only had thoughts about the woman. Our interactions have been nothing short of professional. My thoughts on the other hand—

"I would advise against getting personal with anyone in the class," Deacon says, his eyes focused on me.

"I'm not," I promise, and I think by just saying so it will help keep my mind off her.

Wren's phone chirps a text notification, and he immediately pulls it from his pocket.

"Oh, you naughty girl," he mutters before walking toward his office.

"I need that profile information," Deacon calls to his back.

Wren doesn't say a word before closing himself into his office.

Flynn and Jude chuckle when Deacon shakes his head.

"And why are you drinking double espresso this morning?" I ask my boss when he hits the button on the machine. "Anna still not sleeping well?"

"She's pregnant," he replies as if that's the answer to everything. "But only for a couple more months."

"You won't get much sleep when the baby gets here either," Jude says.

I turn to stare at him.

"What? I read a lot."

"Baby books?" Deacon asks.

"You left one out on the table a couple of weeks ago. Did you know the vagina stretches to—"

"We're not having a conversation about my wife's vagina."

"Not just Anna's, all women," Jude clarifies. "The vagina is a wonderful machine."

"Agreed," Flynn says with a wide smile.

"Perineal massage prior to birth can help prevent tearing. Are you—?"

"Not talking about this with you," Deacon interrupts.

"You're a big guy, man. Can you imagine the size of child she's going to have?" Jude prods, his interest more medical than anything else. "Her—"

"Another word and I'm going to make you help Quinten with the classes," Deacon threatens.

"I'm just saying. All you have to do is rub her—"

"That's it," Deacon snaps.

Flynn tries to hide his laugh behind his fist, but he fails miserably.

"Next class. I want you at the gun range."

I fist pump the air. "Dumbass."

"But—"

"Thursday," Deacon grumbles as he starts to walk away. "Keep talking and I'll make you take them over completely."

I just barely contain a smile as I look over at my best friend. "Class starts at seven sharp. Don't be late."

"I was just trying to be informative. Flynn, wouldn't you want to know if—"

"I have less control than Deacon, so don't even mention Remi's parts."

"Jesus Christ, you guys are Neanderthals!" Jude complains.

"Don't think about his—"

"You either!" Flynn growls with an angry finger pointed in my direction. "If you guys had a woman, you'd understand. Until that happens, just stick to the advice that talking about another man's woman is always a bad idea."

"That went well," I tell my friend as Flynn stands up and walks away. "See you Thursday."

I'm grinning all the way back to my office. Having a little help, or just another dose of testosterone during class can only help, right?

Chapter 8

Hayden

"Are you excited?" I look toward the woman sitting at the table in front of me. "I really thought we'd get to shoot the first class. I hate that we've had to wait until the third."

I give her a weak grin, wondering if she's going to bounce out of her seat with her eagerness.

"I'm Gayle," she continues when I don't give a verbal response.

"Hayden," I say out of courtesy when inwardly I'm cursing Parker for not being here yet.

The door to the classroom opens, and I can't help the frown on my face when I see that it's the instructor rather than Parker. His mouth forms a flat line when he sees me, and I don't know if it's because I've displayed my own disappointment at it not being my friend or if the man really just doesn't like me. I could tell him that he's the one who singled me out that first class and made us leave, but that would only put me on the spot once again. I hate being the center of attention. It's why I don't throw too big of a fit when Parker wants to hang out in public. She draws the attention away from me.

"We're going to start today with learning how to load and unload a magazine," Quinten says the second he's in position at the front of the classroom.

"Aren't we shooting today?" Gayle asks, disappointment evident in her tone.

"Can't shoot without ammunition," he responds. "Magazine size varies. Some only carry a handful of bullets, others can accommodate seventeen or more."

I watch his hands, hating that Parker's conversation about them last week drifts into my head. Quinten holds up each piece as he explains in detail how they work.

"Brand-new magazines are going to be tighter and may hurt your fingers when loading. They get looser the more they're used."

Gayle snorts, obviously taking what he said in a nasty way. Quinten doesn't miss a beat.

"The guys up front can point you to a magazine loader once you decide to buy your own firearm. They'll save the tips of your fingers from pain."

"Sorry I'm late," Parker says as she slides into the seat next to me.

I didn't even hear the classroom door open, and that says a lot about my level of focus on what's going on in the front of the room.

"I can't stay long."

I frown. She's the one who wanted to do this class in the first place, and now she's bailing on me?

"What did I miss?"

"He's showing us how to load that thing with bullets," I answer, my eyes pointed back in Quinten's direction.

"I'm going to pass a couple of these around so you can practice."

"But we don't have guns right now," Gayle complains.

Quinten gives her a wary look. "We're not loading firearms, we're loading magazines. Loaded guns aren't allowed out of the firing range."

"But we are shooting today?"

"Soon," he says as he begins to drop magazines and a handful of bullets on each table. "Remember, the ammunition points out just like I showed you."

His eyes find mine when he's approaches our table, and I have to quickly look away. I don't know what it is about this man that makes me feel so awkward and weird.

Yeah, okay. I can admit that he's handsome, even though I denied it the first time I saw him, but lots of men are attractive. I don't feel my face flush around every good-looking guy I come across, but with him, a simple look in my direction and I can feel the rush of heat on my skin. At first, I chalked it up to my irritation with how he treated me during the first class, but I haven't been upset about that since he showed such care and patience with me last week when I didn't want to pick up the gun, and again when he was worried after class that I hadn't found one I was completely comfortable with.

"Sweet," Parker says as she reaches for the items he's put in front of us, and the spell is broken.

I watch my best friend as she follows his instructions.

Of course, I glance back at him just in time to see him walk away. Parker was right, his jeans are absolutely lethal.

Parker clears her throat, and I see her grinning when I look back at her.

"Your turn," she says as she pops the bullets free. She doesn't mention catching me looking at the man's ass, but I know the reprieve won't last forever. Maybe it's a good thing she can't stay for the entire class. It means I won't be grilled later or forced to go get drinks.

"Sorry I'm late," comes another male voice from the back of the room.

Every woman, including myself, turns our heads as a handsome man begins to walk toward the front of the classroom.

Chatter begins before the man can make it halfway there.

"Everyone this is my co-instructor Jude—"

"Hey Jude!" Gayle sings and I chuckle at her obvious Beatles reference.

"—Jude Morris," Quinten says as if he hadn't been interrupted, but I see a hint of a smile on his face.

Jude gives an awkward wave before shoving his hands into his pockets. The apples of his cheeks begin to turn pink when Quinten claps him on the back.

"He's got a Dr. Reid vibe going on, doesn't he?" Parker whispers right in my ear.

"He looks nothing like Matthew Gray Gubler." I was an avid fan of the television show *Criminal Minds*, but the break-in at my house managed to make me too afraid to watch it. The plotline became a little too real after experiencing that.

"No, like his demeanor. Anyway, do you think Quinten will help if I act like I don't understand how to load this thing?" Parker picks up the magazine and turns it over in her hand.

"He passed the needy slash confused girl test last week. Shouldn't you move on to the next one?"

"I'm thinking a little help would be fun right now." I shake my head before pulling the magazine from her hand and picking up one of the bullets. "Unless you're interested in him. Don't think I didn't catch the way you were looking at his ass. I don't know that I've ever seen you drooling over a man before."

"I wasn't drooling," I mutter, popping the bullet into place and reaching for the next one.

She doesn't argue. Quinten moving around the room to help those that are struggling draws all of her attention.

***

"The entire point of taking a shooting class is to shoot the gun," Parker says as she meets me on the sidewalk outside of the same bar we came to last week.

"And I thought you said you couldn't stay the whole class. Must not have been very important plans."

She doesn't give me any details about what she's missing out on as she curls her arm around mine.

"And how did I end up getting talked in to coming back here?"

"Everyone is coming," Parker says as she pulls open the door for us to walk in.

"Everyone?"

"Is that a little hint of hope I hear in your voice, Hayden Prescott? Don't worry, I invited the guys, so you may have the chance to talk to Dr. Reid tonight."

"Jude Morris," I correct, frowning when she winks at me.

She knew I'd fall for that. Damn it.

"Drink?"

"Just a diet soda for me. The martini last week left me with a headache," I tell her.

Actually, I'm sure the pain behind my eyes had more to do with my lack of sleep than anything else, but I'm not going to risk it again this week.

"Go grab that huge booth over there, so we have room for more people." My eyes follow the point of her finger, and as much as I hate going over there alone, I shove that annoyance down and do as she says.

It seems a little busier tonight, and I studiously avoid looking around the bar.

"Are you having a good night?"

I look up to see a man standing at the edge of the table. He's smiling down at me with a half-empty bottle of beer in his hand.

"I'm good, thanks."

"I couldn't believe my luck when I saw you sit down all alone. My name is—"

"She's not alone."

Both of our heads snap in the direction of the rough voice. I frown at Quinten, somehow grateful for saving me from this guy but also annoyed at the same time.

The guy, on the other hand, cowers back like a kicked puppy. His head literally dips like he's about to be swatted with a rolled-up newspaper for being disobedient.

The guy scurries away as Quinten takes a seat on the far opposite side of the half-moon booth. Jude grabs a chair from an empty table and pulls it up to the edge of our area.

"Maybe I wanted to talk to him."

"I'm good, thanks," he says in an attempted fake female voice. His own voice is so deep, it doesn't work at all. "Didn't exactly sound like you were receptive."

"I don't sound like that, and even if I didn't want to speak with him, it's not your place to run men off when they try to speak to me. I can handle myself."

He smiles at me, and I want to smack the infuriating condescension from his handsome face—*not handsome, Hayden*—just face.

"I'll keep that in mind for next time."

"You're assuming there will be a nex—"

"Hey, how did you beat us here?"

At Parker's voice, I notice both guys are holding cold beers.

"Scoot." Parker nudges Quinten's side with her hip, but he doesn't budge.

He looks up at her like she's lost her mind before standing with a flourish of his arm to indicate her sitting on the inside.

"So gallant," she says with a flutter of her eyelashes.

I would laugh if I hadn't been a witness to her over-the-top flirting before.

"I don't exactly fit comfortably under the table," Quinten says as he settles back on the edge of the seat. Parker hasn't given him much room, and I know that is purposeful.

I glare at my friend, but instead of a conspiratorial smile, she's angling her head, darting her eyes toward Jude. The man hasn't said a word since he arrived. It's clear he's about as comfortable as I am in situations like this.

Parker's eyes widen when I don't open my mouth. I imagine in her head, Jude is the perfect guy for me, and I can admit he's good looking, but I don't feel a spark when I look at him.

Granted, right now, I only feel a little irritation when I look at Quinten, but then that changes when I watch him lift his beer bottle to his lips. I dash away the image of licking that drop of beer left behind on his lip. I don't even like beer. His tongue would taste like hops, and his fingers would be cold from touching the glass bottle.

"Are you okay?" Jude asks.

"Wh-what?"

Parker chuckles, and Quinten shifts in his seat.

"You made like a grunting noise. Is something wrong?"

"I'm fine," I snap, giving Jude a weak smile in apology. "So, you work with Mr. Lake?"

"Mr. Lake," Quinten grumbles as he shakes his head.

"We both work at Blackbridge Security," Jude confirms.

The conversation stays just as stilted as other women from the class begin to trickle in. They hover closely but don't really insert themselves into the four-person group we created.

The ice melts in my soda before I remember that Parker brought me a drink. When I nibble on the straw, Quinten watches me. When I trace my finger down the condensation on the glass, Quinten watches me. When Parker flirts with him, Quinten watches me.

I feel his eyes on me all night long, but not once does he speak directly to me unless I ask him a question first.

The scrutiny in his gaze makes me self-conscious, and I find myself pushing my hair behind my ear more than once just to have something to do with my hands.

He watches me do that, too.

"Ready to go?" I ask Parker after an hour in the booth.

"Already?" She frowns but moves out of the booth when Quinten stands.

"See you guys next week," I mumble before turning toward the door.

I'm outside breathing in fresh air before I realize that both men followed us out.

"Just making sure you get to your car safely," Quinten says when I give him a questioning look.

Suddenly, I don't want to leave. I don't know if it's because the noise from the bar is trapped behind the heavy door or if it's because I'm actually going to miss him looking at me.

"Goodnight," I tell them. "It was nice to meet you, Jude."

Jude gives me a quick nod.

My throat is dry when I look at Quinten, and I regret not sucking down the remainder of my drink before coming out here.

"Drive safely," he says. I might be mistaken but his voice sounds a little huskier than I've heard it.

I resist the urge to hug him because that would be weirder than anything else I've experienced tonight. Parker gives me a weird look over the roof of my car before she opens her driver's side door.

I slide into my car and pull away before she leaves because I don't know when the thought of her talking to Quinten started making me feel a little territorial and jealous.

Chapter 9

Quinten

I sigh after Parker gets in her car and drives away.

"You told Deacon you weren't going to date one of the women from class," Jude says as we stand outside of the bar.

"I'm not."

"Does Parker know that?"

I huff a small laugh because Parker isn't even on my radar.

"She's smoking hot, man. I'd completely understand."

"I don't have eyes for Parker."

"She's got eyes for you. I don't think she stopped watching your mouth the entire night."

"I didn't notice." How could I when I found it impossible to pull my eyes from Hayden?

I don't think she was purposely trying to drive me crazy with her straw or her fingers, or the way she smiled when Jude actually opened his mouth to speak, but she did it anyway.

I left class annoyed with her but planning to try to grab a second alone to speak with her. The invite to the bar from her friend was just lucky. She didn't fire a single gun tonight, and because the group is too large, something I told Wren more than once, I never got a chance to approach her and encourage her to fire.

I thought of offering her private lessons, wondering if the setting and being around so many other people is what made her nervous, but I shoved that idea down before I stupidly made the offer. Being alone with her probably wouldn't be a good thing for either of us.

I can't help but get the feeling that there's more going on than what Wren says she was flagged for, and just imagining someone hurting her makes me homicidal.

"You should've danced with her."

"Hayden doesn't seem like the dancing type."

I look at my friend when he laughs. "I freaking knew it! You have the hots for Hayden, not Parker."

I shake my head, but I don't deny it.

"You spent the entire night talking to her."

Entire isn't actually accurate. Jude spoke when spoken to. He's not rude. He's just not the type to instigate conversations with people he doesn't know. It takes the man a while to warm up to people, and after that, you can't get him to shut up, hence, the reason he was in class tonight. I think his intelligence bothered people growing up, and instead of fostering his knowledge, he was made fun of for it. Staying quiet is like a failsafe for him.

"Are you jealous? I wasn't hitting on Hayden. If I were going to go after either of them, it would be Parker."

"The woman who talks incessantly?"

He shrugs. "She could carry the conversation, but we aren't talking about Parker. Let's talk about Hayden. She's very pretty."

"She is," I agree, knowing my best friend won't give up even if I try to steer the conversation a different way. The best way to get over a conversation is going right through the middle of it.

"She's tiny, though. I don't know how it would work."

With soft hands and practiced skill. With her on top and my hands gripping her hips in case she thinks about biting off more than she can chew. I'd hit the end of her every single time, looking for that little whimper I've never actually heard her make but I've dreamed about more than once.

"Are you thinking about it right now?"

"No," I say a little too quickly not to be guilty.

"You are!"

"I'm not interested in either of them," I lie. "They're clients."

"Do you really think Deacon would give you shit if you started dating Hayden?"

"It's a moot point. Did you miss it when I just said I'm not interested?"

"Did you forget that I'm your best friend, and I know when you're full of shit? Deacon is married to Anna. Flynn and Remi are together. Both of those women were clients. Wren's relationship and his obsession with Whitney started at work. All we do is work. Deacon can't get mad if that's the only way we meet women."

"Are you trying to justify some make-believe crush you think I have on Hayden or that sparkle in your eyes when you say Parker's name?"

His smile grows to twice its original size. "Man, if I thought for even a second I had a shot with Parker, I'd jump on the opportunity to take her out. She's gorgeous."

"There's more to women than just looks."

"Did you not hear her tonight?"

"I wasn't paying attention."

"Because Hayden was in the room. Look, I understand, but Parker isn't a simpleton. She's very smart. Her vocabulary is top notch. Her reasoning skills are on point, The woman is smart."

"If she's as brilliant as you're making her sound, then she should be able to take a hint that I'm not interested," I argue as I start walking toward my truck.

"She's well aware you aren't interested. I think she's trying to make Hayden realize she likes you."

"What?" I spin around so fast I nearly knock him over.

"Not interested, huh?"

"What are we, in high school? Just drop it." Please don't drop it because I want to know what I missed.

"I'm not Brooks," he blessedly continues even though I told him not to. "But I know when a woman is put off and when they're interested. Did you see the way she looked up at you when she was putting her hair behind her ear? Classic flirty move."

"Are you getting your information from *How to Date For Dummies*? She did that because it kept falling in her face and tickling her chin."

I can't believe I was overly eager, and that's the tidbit of information he has? Waste of my damn time.

"There's a *How to Date for Dummies*?"

I laugh at his question, but don't mention his awkwardness.

"I'm going home," I mutter as I hit my key fob and unlock my truck door.

"Yeah, okay. See you at the office."

I give him a wave, but the asshole is right. Home isn't where I want to be, and instead of driving in that direction, I arrow my truck right to the Blackbridge offices. I know he's going to bring up tonight to anyone there that will listen, and I figure being here would give me a little more control over the conversation.

I stop off to grab some fast food, wondering what Hayden had for dinner before heading to work. I realize how random the thought is, especially since I haven't really had a second alone with the woman.

The guys are already laughing when I enter the breakroom with my paper bag filled with cheeseburgers and fries. Yes burgers—plural—because I'm a big guy and can put away some food.

"Any chance I can give you assholes a burger in exchange for shutting up and letting me eat in peace?"

"We already ate," Brooks says as he points between himself and Kit.

"I'll take one," Jude says, holding his hands out in front of him like he's getting ready to catch a football.

He laughs loudly when I narrow my eyes.

"I was just telling the guys about your crush on Hayden."

"Fucker," I mutter, tossing him a burger.

He doesn't open his mouth to talk about the woman again until after he's sank his teeth into the food.

"She's adorable," Jude says around a bite of food. "A tiny little thing, like small enough he could fit her in his pocket. He couldn't take his eyes off her the entire night."

"You going to hit that?" Brooks asks.

The man is a huge flirt and has had his share of women. He's never been in a real relationship that I know of, but he leaves them satisfied, and is somehow able to walk away with them smiling.

"I'm not hitting anything," I say before taking a bite so big that I couldn't talk even if I wanted to.

They either don't notice or don't care about my reluctance.

"You need a good woman in your life. It's been a while since you've been on a date."

"I date," I mumble around partially chewed food.

Brooks scrunches his nose, always the one to have perfect manners. But wouldn't good manners include not talking with a full mouth as well as dropping a topic of conversation when someone isn't wanting to talk?

"When was the last time you were on a date?"

"I had coffee last week."

"You mean the business meeting with Mr. Palmer? Is there something you've failed to tell us, because if you're counting that as a date..." I glare at Brooks, hating that his grin only seems to be getting bigger.

"I'm not gay," I say after forcing down the food in my mouth. I take a smaller bite next because it doesn't seem they're going to let me off the hook whether I'm eating or not.

"But you can't recall the last time you went on a date?" Jude asks, holding out his hand. "Napkin."

I all but growl at him as I reach into the paper sack and shove a napkin in his direction.

"I work a lot."

"We all do," Brooks counters. "But I manage to find time to date."

"You have sex. That's not dating," Jude says.

I point to my best friend in agreement.

"So you're having sex, but you're not dating?" Brooks asks genuinely confused. "And I date. I don't always just meet up for sex."

"You don't?" I ask.

"A man's got to eat." He winks at me in a slimy way, and I have to shake my head at his antics.

"Got mustard in your beard, man. Just right there." I wipe at my mouth, scowling at Brooks. "Other side, idiot."

"Fuck off," I hiss as I wipe both sides of my mouth.

"Does that beard get in the way when you're eating pussy?"

Jude snorts at Brooks's question, finding it funny, but his cheeks still turn a little red. He's never been very comfortable talking about sex.

"Many women like a little scruff burn on the insides of their thighs," Wren says, walking into the room and jumping right into the conversation.

"That's true," Brooks agrees. "But it may be a little much. Maybe trim it up some."

"It doesn't get in the way, and if Hayd—I have no intentions of eating pussy any time soon."

"Wow. Freudian slip? Wishful thinking?" Brooks taunts.

"Do you have the hots for Hayden Prescott? The woman in your shooting class?" Wren asks.

"No."

"Yes." Jude counters my lie.

"Can you ever keep your mouth shut?" I snap at my best friend.

I don't know if I'm mad because he's gossiping like a teen girl in the school bathroom or if the topic of conversation has me wondering just how into the scrape of my beard on her thigh Hayden would be.

"We're all family," he mutters as he crinkles up his trash before throwing it at my head.

"Really? Why don't you tell your family about the last time you had sex?"

His eyes flare.

"Interesting," Wren says. "Tell us, Jude."

"Why are we talking about sex?"

"You're the one who came in here running your mouth about a client from the shooting class."

"Tell us," Wren prods. "Do you use your medical supplies? Are you kinky?"

"I told you that in confidence," Jude hisses.

"You told me that years ago," I remind him. His eyes dart to a spot across the room. "What? Really? No. Still?"

"Fuck, I need popcorn," Brooks says, clapping his hands like a hungry baby seeing a box of Cheerios. "Explain."

Jude doesn't answer. I immediately register the change in his breathing. He's embarrassed. Fuck, I didn't mean for that to happen. It agitates me a little that they're being nosy about Hayden, but his secrets are much bigger than that. It's my turn to be surprised because this is not the direction I thought this conversation was going. I regret opening my stupid mouth.

"We're all waiting, Jude," Wren pressures.

"Leave him alone. It's nothing." Neither Wren nor Brooks looks in my direction.

"Oh, wow. You haven't, have you?" Wren asks, but his tone is serious not teasing. "Dude, that—"

"You're a virgin?" Brooks asks, his mouth hanging open in shock. "That's—"

"Fucking awesome," Wren says in admiration.

"Like ever?" Brooks continues, still baffled.

"Go ahead," Jude says glaring at me, angry for spilling the beans before looking over at the other guys. "Make fun of me."

"Why?" Brooks asks, his brow creasing. "I mean, I'm not saying I would give up all of my experiences just to have sex again for the first time, but—"

"I would," Wren snaps. "In a fucking heartbeat. If the only woman I ever put my mouth on or stuck my co—had sex with was Whitney, I could die a happy man. I didn't lose my virginity until I was twenty-one so it's no big deal. You're what, twenty-four?"

I roll my lips between my teeth to keep from smiling.

"Thirty-one," he mutters, his eyes darting quickly away.

Brooks hands clap over his head as he falls back into a reclining position on the sofa. "I don't understand."

"You're a total virgin?" Wren asks with the disclosure of Jude's age.

"Why is this such a big deal?" Jude asks, but his scowl is starting to fade with the realization that the guys aren't going to make fun of him.

"Virgins just don't exist these days. Most people lose it in high school, and if not then, they do in college."

"We moved around a lot. Military brat, remember?" Jude explains.

"There were no girls or guys on base?" Brooks asks.

"Not gay," Jude clarifies.

"You sure? I mean if you haven't—"

"I'm sure," Jude interrupts.

"So no girls on base?" Brooks continues as Wren drops his ass down to the arm of the couch, looking at my friend like a science experiment or a new computer program he doesn't quite understand.

"We moved a lot. There was no time to really get to know anyone."

"I'm going home," I say as I stand, gathering my trash.

"We're not done talking about Hayden and the way you watched her all night," Jude says to my back.

"We'll get to that later," Wren says. "So like nothing? Never gotten a blow job, never given a girl head, like nothing?"

I walk out and leave my friend right in the middle of the spotlight he flipped the switch on and turned in my direction.

I'll apologize later, but for now, I need a little distance from it all.

Chapter 10

Hayden

"All night," Parker says as she presses the bullets into the magazine. "I was talking to him and he was watching you. I'm telling you, the man has it bad for you."

"What? No, he wasn't."

He was, and apparently I wasn't the only one to notice his undivided attention despite not really engaging with him last week at the bar.

"Besides, you like him so even if he was, it doesn't matter."

"What are you talking about? Like him? I don't like him."

I glare at her. "Seriously?"

"Has that been what's holding you back?"

"I'm not holding back. I—"

"Hold that thought." Parker turns around and fires the gun, hitting the target several times. "Don't tell me you don't like him. The man is fucking gorgeous."

"You ladies okay down here?"

The air feels thick and I know it has more to do with Quinten's approach than the slight haze of smoke from so many guns being fired at the same time.

I flinch when the woman in the third lane takes her first shot, and it doesn't go unnoticed by Quinten.

"Have you picked it up yet?" He looks over at the gun that felt the least uncomfortable in my hands. It's still in the basket the attendant at the front handed to me in when I checked it out.

"I'm just not feeling it," I tell him with a raised voice.

"Is it awkward? Because it always is at first. Pick it up and let me check your grip."

"Maybe show us how you hold yours," Parker suggests, and the flirty tone in her voice makes me want to step on her toe just to get her to back up a few inches.

Quinten nods before pulling his own gun from the holster on his hip. He pops out the magazine and does this sexy thing where he pulls back the top, making the bullet inside it fly out. He catches it gracefully.

"Are you watching?" I nod, catching myself a second too late, before biting the corner of my bottom lip.

His eyes track the movement before he shifts a little further away.

I watch as he pops the single bullet back into the clip before sliding it into place in the gun. He pulls the top back. Crap, if I were paying attention to his words in class instead of the sure movements of his hands, I would know what that part is called.

"Like this. Keep both thumbs facing forward. Stand like this so you're more stable. The gun you picked out doesn't have the power to knock you over, despite what you might have seen on online videos."

I nod, watching his strong legs bend ever so slightly at the knee.

"So just a little bend?" Parker asks. "Or a lot. What's too far?"

"You want to be like this." Quinten turns to face the target before squatting a little lower. "Going this far down isn't practical, and it's not something you'd do in a real-life situation."

"Jesus," Parker says before biting her fist. She pulls it out quickly, looking down at her hand like it tastes disgusting.

I huff a laugh at her ridiculousness.

"Jesus, Hay. Look at that. I bet he could squeeze a gala apple between those cheeks and make pulp free apple juice."

"That's enough," Quinten says. He reholsters his gun and turns to glare at my friend. "This is a serious class, and the commentary isn't needed."

Parker's mouth hangs open. "What?"

"You aren't exactly whispering, and it's clear you don't know this, but," he points to his headset, "these are electronic, which means I can hear you just fine. Even when you think you're whispering."

My lips twitch as I try to keep from laughing. It isn't often that my best friend gets embarrassed. She hasn't said anything to me that she wouldn't say to his face, but she very rarely gets called out.

"Hayden." Quinten sweeps his hand in the direction of the basket holding my rented gun. "Your turn."

"I'm not ready to shoot."

"Okay. That's fine. I want to see you practice your stand and hold."

I move to the head of the lane and pull the gun and clip from the basket.

"Check and make sure it's loaded."

"It's not," I tell him.

"Because you already checked it?"

"Because the guy at the counter wouldn't give it to me that way."

"Humans make mistakes. You can see the magazine isn't in. Now to check the chamber, pull back on the slide and look inside. Good. Is it empty?"

"Yes," I answer, wishing he was a little closer to me. For selfish reasons, of course, not because of fear of the gun or anything.

That's a lie. I'm terrified of shooting. I'm afraid of the recoil like he mentioned. I'm afraid of the bang. I'm afraid of looking like a fool because I do it wrong. If I were rich, I'd hire a full-time bodyguard to stand at my bedroom door while I slept because I'm exhausted and that makes me emotional. And being emotional makes me angry because I should have better control over myself.

The gun starts to shake in my hands.

I clear my throat, muttering under my breath motivational things like—you're doing great, Hayden. You got this. Don't be scared.

"You don't have to be scared. Here. Move this one down just a little. When you shoot for real, you're going to end up with slide burn if you're that high."

Now I have to worry about the individual parts of the gun hurting me?

Jesus, I may just not even show up to the next two classes.

I can't even focus on the fact that he heard my not so flowery affirmations.

"Pull the slide back, point, aim and shoot."

"It's not loaded," I remind him.

"I know, but get used to the click before worrying about the boom."

Quinten takes a step back, not saying another single word to me as I get in position and do as he says. I flinch the first time I get the courage to squeeze the trigger, but after I realize that it isn't going to jump out of my hands, I find it easier to repeat.

Quinten goes to help someone else while Parker and I trade off, her using a loaded weapon and me clicking mine a handful of times.

I tell Parker I'm staying behind, thinking maybe shooting in an empty room would be easier if I don't have any witnesses if I look stupid. When class is over, I head to the front and wait my turn to step up to the counter. The guy doesn't bat an eye when I tell him that I want to re-rent the gun and purchase a box of practice ammunition.

The transaction is smooth, and I'm feeling a little more confident when I step into the firing lane alone, but my throat is still dry. I check the gun, just like Quinten instructed even though it was never out of my sight and I cleared it before leaving the room the first time.

Instead of loading an empty magazine, I slide bullet after bullet into the magazine until it's full, but then I find my hands shaking again when I pick it up to slide it into position.

It takes another five minutes of me staring down at the thing, legs quaking a little before I slide the magazine home, and another three minutes before I pull the slide back to move that first bullet into position. When that is done, I lay the thing back down, making sure that the muzzle is pointed down range at all times like he mentioned during my first full class.

After several long breaths, I pick it back up, terror filling my blood and making my forehead sweat a little.

I'm trying to talk myself into actually going through with it when I hitch my shoulder to attempt to catch a bead of sweat rolling down at my temple, and then the damn thing just goes off in my hand.

Chapter 11

Quinten

"Thanks as always," I tell Adam, tapping the doorframe of his office before leaving for the night. "I turned off the lights in the classroom."

"What are you teaching these women?"

My mind goes straight to Gayle who was shockingly absent in class today, but then I look past him at the video monitor on his desk.

"She spent ten minutes at what looked like psyching herself up to shoot. She fires off a single shot. I can't be one hundred percent sure, but I don't even think she did that one on purpose, and now, for five minutes, she's been standing like that."

Hayden is standing at lane three with her head lowered and her hands on her hips.

"She pulled the trigger?"

"I saw the brass eject, but I don't think it was on purpose."

"Hmm." Maybe she did just need to be alone to do it the first time.

"See that shake?" he asks, pointing to the screen when she picks the gun back up. "I better go see if she needs some help."

I clamp a hand on his shoulder before he can fully stand. "I'll do it."

"Quickly," he urges. "Before she hurts herself."

The room is empty except for her, so she can hear when I open the door and join her. Since leaving Adam's office, she's laid the gun back down, resuming her stance with her hands on her hips. When she turns to face me, I notice that her forehead is damp, but there's a soft smile on her face.

"I shot it."

"And it scared you so badly, you're terrified to do it again?"

She nods. "Does that make me a wuss?"

"Not in the least. It's a deadly weapon. It's good that you respect it as such, but I don't want you to be afraid of it either. Turn around and pick it back up."

She does, and her hands are either trembling more now or the video didn't capture the full shake earlier.

"Hold on," I tell her, placing my hand on top of her forearms, so she lowers the gun. "Look at me."

I slide my hand down to hers and take the other one lightly in mine as well.

"Relax." I move her hands making her arms shake. "Take a deep breath. It's like jumping off a cliff into the lake for the first time. It's perfectly normal to be a little nervous."

"I've never jumped off a cliff," she says, making me grin.

Of course she hasn't.

"Now let's try again. Don't lock your knees, but don't slouch. Pick it up. No, like this." Without thought, I step in behind her and wrap my arms around hers, readjusting her hands on the grip. "Does that feel better?"

When she nods her head, the scent of her hair invades my nose, and like a fool, I dip a little lower to get a better whiff, which nearly has me on my damn knees.

With our size difference, I'm not even touching her except where my arms come over hers.

"Tighten up here," I tell her as I trail my fingers up her arms to her elbows. Did she have goosebumps before I touched her? "Perfect."

I take a step back.

"Sorry. I shouldn't have touched you without asking first."

When she turns her head to look at me, the gun comes along for the ride.

"Down range," I snap, startling her.

The gun fires and thank God the bullet goes wide.

She screeches as she drops the gun on the table at her waist. She stares down at the thing like it just insulted her.

"That's twice now that's happened. I'm done. I don't want to do this anymore."

"Twice? That happened the first time you shot in here alone?"

She's shaking, and although I want to lift her chin so I can see her eyes, I keep my distance. She's here to learn how to shoot, not be railroaded by a man who has a tendency to take over and do things himself because it's faster and easier.

"I went to wipe sweat off my face."

"With your right hand?" My eyes widen, knowing she's right-handed. "You could've—"

"With my shoulder." She mimics the motion, lifting her shoulder to the damp side of her face.

"And it went off because your finger was on the trigger just like now. What did I say in class?"

"Don't put your finger on the trigger until you're ready to shoot, and I was ready, then I felt the sweat."

"Then you take your finger off the trigger."

"Obviously, I will from now on."

"Except when someone talks to you? Then it's okay to swing a gun in their direction?"

She narrows her eyes at me, and I know I'm seconds away from getting a good dose of her feisty attitude, but at least she isn't near tears like she was a minute ago.

"Finger off the trigger until you're ready to shoot. If you get distracted, finger off the trigger. Always finger—"

"Off the trigger. Yeah, I got it."

"Good, now turn around and pick it back up."

"I think I'm done."

"You've only shot twice and neither of those times were on purpose. Let's go. Turn around."

Her eyes dart to mine, holding me captive for a long moment before she turns back to face the target ten feet down the range.

"Remember what I said. Put your thumbs like—may I touch you?"

"Please." She shakes her head. "I mean, yes. That's fine."

I'm smiling like a damned fool when I step up behind her for the second time. I have to make sure that I keep my hips back a little further because her verbal slipup is causing my own physical reaction, and I don't think she'd appreciate knowing it if I pressed it against her.

"That can't be comfortable for you," she says as she looks over her shoulder at me.

God, all I'd have to do is brush her hair a few inches to the side, and I'd have access to her neck. I just know the skin there would be soft, scented with her sweet body wash and sweat. I clear my throat as she turns her face back toward the target.

"It's fine." Perfect, actually. "You ready?"

She shakes her head but reaches for the gun anyway.

"Arms to here," I tell her, lifting them a few inches higher. "Good, now move your thumb. Perfect."

Her hands still have a slight tremble in them, but at least the weapon is pointed down range.

"Take a few calming breaths, but then hold it right before you squeeze the trigger. Fire when you're ready."

I've helped her get in position, and there's no reason to stay right behind her, but I don't step back. I don't know that I could.

"One eye open or both?"

"Let's just worry about getting used to pulling the trigger before lining up a shot."

She nods slightly in understanding, the top of her head brushing my beard.

"When you're ready," I repeat as we stand quietly for a few minutes.

She fires. The bullet doesn't puncture the target, but like I told her, we weren't really focusing on that.

"Good. Now again."

It doesn't take her as long to fire the second time, and the third and fourth come in quick succession.

By the time the magazine is empty, her hands shake wildly, but she lowers the gun, placing it on the table in front of her before spinning around with a huge grin on her face. I know the tremble there now is adrenaline and thrill rather than fear.

"How do you feel?"

She swallows. "That was pretty cool."

"Okay. Let's load it back up and do it again."

I step back, not offering to help as she discharges the magazine and begins to reload.

"Who taught you to shoot?"

"The Army."

"Really? How long did you serve?" she asks as she slides the magazine back into the gun too softly, frowning when it pops back out. She hits it a little harder the second time, smiling once again when it clicks into place.

"Eight years. It seems like a lifetime ago."

"Well," she says as she places the gun back on the table to turn to look at me, "thank you for your service."

I give her a quick smile, doing my best at trying not to watch her mouth when she speaks, but her lips are like a beacon, drawing my attention there.

"Are you trying to distract me to keep from shooting?"

She blinks, her pretty eyes flashing with mirth, before turning back around.

"Still need help getting lined up?"

"I think… I'd like some help."

I step back in behind her, only this time when I touch her arms, my hands slide from her elbows to her wrists. I'm close enough to track her change in breathing pattern, and against my better judgment, I end up closer to her this time.

Her first three shots are fine, but the third manages to hit the line holding the target. She gasps as we watch the target flutter to the ground.

"Oh no," she whispers.

"It happens more often than you'd think," I tell her.

Thankfully, she puts the gun down before turning to face me, and I don't immediately move away. We end up standing so close she has to crane her face up to look me in the eye. My fingers twitch to run them down her cheek or cup the back of her neck.

"Am I in trouble?"

I shake my head, words lost to me right now.

"I broke it."

I watch as her eyes dart back and forth between mine, but for the life of me, I can't find my own voice. Has she always been this gorgeous?

"Quinten?" She blinks again. "I'll pay to have it fixed."

"Hit the line?"

Her eyes snap toward Adam's voice as he comes into the room, and it's only then that I'm able to take a step back.

"Yeah," I say, running my hand down my face and over my beard. My lips tingle with unmet need, leaving me feeling like I'm missing something.

"I'm going to walk her to her car. I'll be back to take care of everything." I turn and begin to walk out of the room, unsure if she's even following me.

Chapter 12

Hayden

I sigh in frustration, closing my eyes for a solid minute before I open them again. When I type in the numbers again, it's still wrong.

I've been working on this one account for the last hour, and it isn't adding up. If I ever had a good reason to hate Mondays, this would be one.

I type in the numbers again. I'm coming up with the same total, but the account is still showing a different balance. I flip through invoices, checking those for the fourth time before finally giving in.

After shoving everything on that account into a folder, I head toward my boss's office. He doesn't bother to look up from his own work when I tap on the doorframe. This is nothing new. He's not a jerk, but he's a little aloof most days, focused on his own work.

"I'm having trouble with the Grimsson account."

His head snaps up, and I wonder if maybe he was so fixated on his own work that he didn't hear my knock.

"Why are you working on the Grimsson account?"

I tilt my head in confusion. "Because I'm the accountant."

He holds his hand out, and it takes a few breaths before I realize he's wanting me to hand over the folder.

"Don't worry about this one," he says when it's in his hand. "I'll figure it out. It's a little more complicated than the others."

"Okay," I tell him and turn around to leave before I open my mouth and remind him that I'm very good at my job.

Chances are there's a missing invoice or paperwork that was misfiled because I know my calculations are correct. If the man wants to spend another couple of hours clearing it up, let him.

I grab my purse the second I get to my desk and leave for lunch. If I'm being honest with myself, I've been annoyed since driving away from Quinten Thursday night. One minute, he's a foot away looking down at me like he's barely able to resist pressing his lips to mine, but then he's giving me a rough goodbye from five feet away.

Lunch consists of a quick drive-thru meal because I spent half of my lunch hour trying to get the numbers on that stupid account to add up correctly, but I find time to call Parker to see if she wants to go to the gun range with me after work for practice.

She claims she has to work, but I get the feeling she has other plans. Or maybe I'm just annoyed at being turned down. I hate doing things by myself, but these days, I hate going home alone even more.

When my workday is over, I try not to think about Quinten and the possibility that he might be at the gun range. I mean, the man works for Blackbridge Security, not full-time at the gun range. Even knowing that doesn't keep the disappointment from creeping up when I walk inside and don't see him.

The guy at the counter is a different man from the one who witnessed my embarrassment last week, and he tells me the same thing Quinten did when I broke the line the target was on.

"Don't worry about it. It actually happens all the time."

I give him a weak smile, wanting to blame Quinten for standing so close and making me more nervous about his proximity and how much I enjoyed it than actually firing the gun.

Once I was over the initial fear, pulling the trigger was actually thrilling. I wanted to do it over and over, but that sense of wariness never left. It's why I'm back today. I've always been a good student and doing something and not being able to perfect a skill stresses me out.

I know I'm not going to turn into a gun-slinging badass overnight, but maybe with practice, I can actually hit the target instead of breaking the machines.

There is one other man in lane two when I enter the room and head for lane six. He doesn't even bother to look up at me. I flinch when he shoots, and I wonder if I'll ever stop doing that. I know to expect it, but the sound, even with my protective earmuffs on is startling.

I juggle the basket the gun and ammo are in along with the target, wondering just when I lost confidence in my actions. Even earlier, walking into the building, I nearly tripped over the curb because I was too busy looking around the parking lot. Something about the setting sun and the way shadows danced over the cars in the lot gave me the creeps.

I scoffed at the police officer that came to the house the night of the break-in. She'd handed me a card with information for a local support group for people who had experienced the same type of victimization. I thought it was ridiculous, wondering why people were so anxious about something like that happening to them. Those were thoughts of an angry woman, a woman that was livid that her favorite picture frame was found busted on the living room floor. That woman was ready to go out and look for the man herself.

Then the adrenaline and anger washed away, leaving me with fear and anxiety, and regret for having thrown that card into the trash with the glass from that very picture frame I was so angry about.

There's less tremble in my hands when I load the bullets, and by the time the magazine is in the gun and I have it pointed down range, I'm livid at the fear some stranger has been able to instill in me.

I breathe the way Quinten suggested, holding my breath in the second it takes for me to pull the trigger. I fire over and over, not pausing except to check my breathing until the slide locks back indicating that the magazine is now empty.

I reload and do it all over again.

After the third magazine, I move the target back to me and take pride in every one of the tiny holes in the paper. They're scattered with not even an ounce of consistency, but it's better than every shot going wide. I send the target back down the lane and reload.

I do this several more times until it becomes hard to tell which holes were there from the previous time.

I grow increasingly frustrated that there's no regularity to my shots.

"How's it going?"

I startle, dropping the bullet in my hand when I hear the male voice.

Dropping the magazine, I spin around, only feeling mild comfort when I see Jude's smiling face.

"Hey," I say weakly, for some reason feeling a little weird to be speaking with him without Parker or Quinten around.

"I just came to practice," he explains when I shift awkwardly on my feet. "Do you need any help?"

"I—umm. I can't seem to hit the target every time," I confess.

"Well, finish loading, and I can give you some pointers."

I do as he says, and thankfully he doesn't step in behind me like Quinten did on Thursday. Jude stands to the side, observing as I get in my stance and aim.

"The key to consistency is finding your dominant eye. So look down range with both eyes open and pick a spot on the target. Close one eye and then the other. The eye that maintains the same position of spot is your dominant eye. Practice it now while looking down the sight lines. Good. Now which eye is dominant?"

"The right," I answer after doing what he said a handful of times.

"Okay, now line up that spot with your left eye closed."

"I didn't pick the center of the target," I mutter.

"That's fine. You can practice anywhere on a target to get the most use out of it. That's why those smaller targets are in the corner. When you're ready, fire."

I do as he said, semi-confidently shooting until the magazine is once again empty. I press the button to bring the target back to me, but once again there are so many holes from my previous shooting that I don't know which ones are from this last round.

"Let's get you a new target, and go from there," Jude says, reaching in the lane next to mine and grabbing his target rather than going back out front to get another one.

"A zombie?" I ask, looking down at his target of choice.

He shrugs before handing it over. I like that he doesn't just urge me out of the way to pull my old target and replace it with his. He's really a sweet guy, and nothing like Quinten who is more likely to be found with a scowl on his face rather than a smile.

Too bad I don't feel even a blip of chemistry when he's near, no matter how much Parker tried to push him onto me that night at the bar. I know what she was thinking. He's shy and awkward, and so am I, but that isn't going to work out like she planned.

For some reason, I have a thing, probably fleeting, for his grouchy best friend.

"Ready when you are," Jude says, clearing his throat and making me realize I've just been standing here staring at him.

My face is flushed, and I pray he didn't take the attention the wrong way and turn back to the task at hand.

I want to bounce up and down after emptying the next magazine and counting the holes in the target. I hit it with all but one shot.

He's grinning at my enthusiasm.

"I didn't hit the spot I was shooting at but look!" I count them out as if the man can't see them clearly himself.

"That's great. My only observation is that you're pulling up just a little before each shot because you're anticipating the recoil. After shooting enough, you'll no longer do that and be unstoppable."

I repeat the process until all of my bullets are gone, and each time I get a little better. I'm not a marksman by any definition of the word, but I am more confident. By the last magazine, I hit the target with every shot.

"Thanks so much for your help," I tell him as I place the gun back in the basket to take back to the front. "I owe you a couple targets."

"Don't worry about it," he says, his hand going to the back of his neck as his cheeks turn pink.

Oh God, what do I say if he asks me out?

"So, umm… Your friend, Parker, the one that was at the bar the other night, isn't here today?" he asks as if I have a million friends and need the clarification.

I roll my lips between my teeth to fight a smile. Of course he's going to ask about Parker. Sadly, my best friend would chew this sweet man up and spit him out.

"She had to work," I tell him. "But maybe you'll get the chance to see her Thursday at class."

He nods, his eyes darting away.

"Have a good night."

"Stay safe," he says to my back when I walk away.

The dread I felt walking into the building hits me in the face the second I step outside and rush to my car. The sun has fully set and instead of creepy shadows bouncing around, I'm met with total darkness. I'm left feeling cold and scared once again.

Chapter 13

Quinten

"It's simple, Mr. Dickerson. Stop hiring hookers, and the media will stop reporting that you're hiring hookers."

I sigh into the phone receiver. It seems like great advice to me, but what the hell do I know?

"I think a better solution to the problem would be to sue the news station."

"Because you have a good case for a libel suit?"

"Yes."

"The media is printing lies about you?"

"Well—"

"Last time I checked their site online, they had a video of you picking up a hooker in south St. Louis two nights ago."

"She's a friend of the family," he counters.

"And you have proof of that?"

He remains silent.

"I don't keep records of transactions with hook—I mean friends. Whose side are you on?"

"You're the client, Mr. Dickerson, but you make it hard to help you when you continue to do the same thing over and over."

"It's a free country," he grumbles. "I don't understand why people are concerned with who I spend time with."

I pinch the bridge of my nose, wondering what Deacon would say if I told him that I plan to drop this man as a client. Working with him is seriously starting to make my skin crawl.

"Back to the point at hand. You can't sue the news station if you were, in fact, picking up a prostitute."

"Then I need a different resolution."

"Any suggestions?"

"I need you to find me a reputable escort service."

"Blackbridge Security isn't that type of company. Have you considered using dating apps?"

"I don't have time for that shit."

I don't have time for your shit.

"We're not going to find you an escort service, Mr. Dickerson, and I don't know that our services are right for you if that's the expectation. I'll forward your case information to Mr. Black, and we can go from there."

"It's an honest transaction. I'm not forcing them to get in the car with me. The sex industry—"

"Is illegal in St. Louis."

"But it shouldn't be!" he hisses, so loudly I have to pull the phone from my ear.

"I can't fix a reputation you continue to tarnish."

"I hired you assholes to—"

"Goodbye, Mr. Dickerson. Mr. Black will be in contact soon."

I hang up the phone before he can continue to rant.

Leaning back in my office chair, I stare at the ceiling. The days just continue to drag on and on, and I know it's because I'm forced to wait from one Thursday to the next to see Hayden.

"That's the look of a man who isn't having the best day," Deacon says as he steps into my office.

"We're going to have to drop Dickerson," I tell him.

"Still hiring prostitutes?"

"He wants us to find him a reputable escort service."

Deacon scoffs at the ridiculous request. "Tell the man to move to Nevada. There are several counties there that it's legal. How bad is it this time?"

"He made the evening news yesterday." Deacon frowns. "And before you ask, they have it on video. He's in breach of contract."

"I'll contact him," he says as he drops another handful of folders on my desk. "Let's talk about these real quick."

I flip through the first folder as Deacon sits in the chair across from my desk. The case notes indicate a dad going after his daughter's boyfriend for posting her nudes to a high school chatroom.

"Child porn? That would be easy to solve, but we have to worry about making things worse by bringing to light that she—"

"She's eighteen. A senior in high school, so that doesn't fit."

"Revenge porn? I have no desire to look at the images sent. Does it show her face?"

"Full frontal in a bathroom mirror," Deacon confirms. "But I'm not concerned about the case against the boy who shared them. The father hurt him pretty badly. The boy is the preacher's son from the dad's church. The congregation is up in arms, defending the boy, while ostracizing the girl for sending the pictures in the first place. Apparently, she's the temptress, and the boy is just another unwilling victim."

"I might believe that shit if the preacher found the images instead of his son spreading them around. Let me guess, the boy was doing God's work by letting everyone know who to avoid? God, I hate double standards."

We continue to talk about this case and the other three he's shoved my way this morning before he gets up to leave. Despite having a ton of work to get done, the day doesn't go by any faster. I find myself continuously looking up at the clock on the wall.

After setting a game plan for three of the cases with the clients and waiting for the fourth to call me back, I make my way to the breakroom.

Jude is on the sofa, playing with that stupid length of rope. Kit is cleaning a handgun. Wren is nowhere to be seen and probably in his office jacking off and giving filthy commands to his woman over a video call.

All seems normal around here.

"Where have you been?" Jude asks when he notices me.

"Working. You should try it sometime."

"The team has been injury free for eighteen days," Jude responds.

"Great. You had to say it out loud?" Flynn complains. "Now you've jinxed us."

"I don't conform to your superstitions," Jude tells him before looking back at me. "Did I tell you that I ran into Hayden?"

He laughs when my body tenses. "You didn't. When? Today? Is she here?"

"Interesting," Kit says. "Is this the girl from the shooting class?"

It doesn't surprise me that he's gotten details on a conversation he wasn't even present for.

"It was yesterday at the gun range," Jude explains.

"Classes are on Thursday."

"And the range is open seven days a week." Jude's eyes narrow. "She mentioned you telling her to not worry about aim for now."

Flynn chuckles. Kit huffs a laugh.

It's clear with both their reactions that they know exactly what I did.

"She was scared of the gun," I argue, unwilling to confess the truth.

"And you're well aware that starting with all the fundamentals— including aim—is pertinent," Kit says.

I frown but keep my eyes on Jude, hoping he'll tell me how she's doing without me actually having to ask the damned question.

"So you sandbagged her, so she'd be more likely to ask for more help." Flynn explains my intentions out loud, and I can only guess how ridiculous it sounds to these guys. "If I had to guess, I bet you stood behind her and physically positioned her arms, didn't you?"

They all laugh when I clamp my mouth closed.

"Pitiful, man. Just pitiful."

Jude's smile grows at Kit's reaction. "I know you're too stubborn to ask, so I'll tell you that she looked good."

She always looks good, I want to say.

"What was she wearing?" My eyes snap to Flynn. I'm seconds away from knocking the cheesy grin off his face.

"Very feminine slacks, and—" If he mentions a blouse, I'm likely to punch my best friend in the face. "A flowy top. It looked like silk."

"Jude," I warn. It's the only one he'll get.

Another round of laughter comes from Flynn as he stands. "Just ask the woman out already. Maybe it'll put an end to that hostility you're feeling grow in your chest."

I think hitting each one of them for having a good time at my expense also sounds like a viable option.

"She's getting better," Jude says. "I helped her establish eye dominance, and by the end of the lane rental she—"

"Quinten, I have another case to discuss with you," Deacon says as he walks into the room, interrupting a vital conversation.

Jude snaps his mouth closed, refusing to continue. I walk away, working through how to get the information out of him later. He's having fun with this right now, but eventually I'll get him to spill. I'm barely able to pay attention to Deacon once we're back in his office going over the file.

Never in my life has someone been able to make me lose focus so easily. Maybe Flynn is right and asking her out would be the best way to go. More likely than not, I'll spend a little time with her and realize we aren't compatible, or she'll shoot me down, and I'll know exactly where I stand with her.

Thursday can't get here soon enough.

Chapter 14

Hayden

The second to last class is wrapping up, and I don't know if I'm anxious because Parker didn't show up at all or if it's because I don't want them to end.

It could also be because I have to once again go home to a house I no longer feel safe in. Exhaustion is weighing down on me, but when I close my eyes at night, I can't sleep. It's making me irritable to the point I snapped at someone at work earlier today for something that normally wouldn't cause my blood pressure to spike in the slightest. I apologized profusely, but felt guilty for the rest of the day.

"How are you feeling about it now?" Quinten asks.

The attention I'm getting right now is nothing different from what he's offered to every other woman in the class, but I bask in it, slowing my response time to make it last just a little longer.

At first sight, I judged this man as angry and frightening because of his size and the way he holds his mouth in a nearly constant frown, but the more I look at him and watch him, that opinion changes. I find him giving small smiles of approval when someone celebrates their success with shooting. He's quick to give compliments at a job well done, and he's a true instructor, explaining and showing when there are issues rather than getting upset and agitated when one of us can't do what he's suggesting the first time.

"Hayden?"

"Yes, I'm getting the hang of it. Jude's advice earlier this week helped a lot, too."

He nods, that information not coming as a surprise to him. Does that mean they were talking about me?

I get a small twinge of excitement at imagining them talking about me outside of class. Does it mean he's interested, or is he just being polite?

"Let's see your target."

I stand to the side as he recalls the target, and I diligently keep my eyes from noticing the fit of his jeans. If Parker were here, she probably would've mentioned them more than once, giving me the ability to look without feeling so weird, but she once again had to work.

"The clusters are getting tighter. Are you aiming at different areas with each magazine?"

"Yes," I answer. "Jude suggested it."

He clears his throat before turning back around to face me. "That's good advice. Are you coming often to practice outside of class?"

"Just on Monday."

"You're coming every Monday?"

It feels as if he's asking while mentally making plans to clear his schedule in a couple of days.

"I plan to. After work. I'll get here about six thirty." My face flames at giving him too much information, but he nods as if he's filing it away.

"The more you're able to practice, the better you'll get. In the beginning, going longer between shooting may set you back to the beginning. Good job."

He hands me the target and moves on to the next lane.

Disappointed the interaction is over, I gather my things and head out to the front, but after checking my rental back in, I find myself reluctant to walk out of here.

Each day, the fear of going home alone and of being watched grows instead of getting better. Time has done nothing but make my anxiety ramp up. Maybe coming every day to shoot after work is better than just once a week because at least I can postpone the racing heart I get each night as I pull up to my house.

I spend twenty minutes looking at the products the shop has to offer, stupidly reading the backs of the items without really understanding the purpose of them.

"Are you waiting on someone?"

Like a fool, I nearly drop the bottle of gun oil I've been holding as I look up at Quinten.

"Just, ah, shopping."

"Most people use oil, not grease."

"What?" My brow draws together in confusion until he points to the product in my hand. "Oh. Good to know."

I know I don't like being around lots of people, but when did I become unable to carry on a normal one-on-one conversation with a man?

I shake my head at how ridiculous I'm acting.

"It's not included in the class, but I can teach you how to take a gun apart and clean it."

I shake my head.

"Or the guys here can do it for you."

"I haven't decided what I want." Honestly, I don't know that I'll ever actually buy a gun. Learning to shoot hasn't built up much confidence, and I don't imagine carrying a gun around on my person would help that either.

"The offer stands when you do."

Even if the class is over? Am I confident enough to call this man up and hold him to it? Probably not.

"Okay. Well, thanks."

Those three words should be enough for me to walk away, but I find myself lingering. He patiently waits, and if I was better at interacting with men I find attractive, I might think he wanted to stick around, too, but I'm not.

"You seem hesitant to leave. Is there something wrong?"

What a loaded question, and I pause for a minute wondering if spilling my fears and anxiety at this man's feet is the best thing to do.

He did ask after all.

"My house was broken into," I say, my eyes dropping to my shoes.

"That's rough."

I huff. "You have no clue. I changed the locks, but I still..."

"Having trouble feeling safe?"

Did he just close some of the distance between us, or am I swaying on my feet?

"It's worse than I thought it was going to be. I'm having trouble sleeping."

"What about an alarm system?"

I shake my head. "I've called, but the companies I contacted are busy. I'm on a few waitlists, but then I also worry about the company having access to my codes, and I'm probably just being paranoid, but—"

"No. It's a legitimate concern."

And that little piece of information doesn't make me feel any better.

"Maybe you could—"

"Do you want to go for coffee?" I blurt.

His upper lip twitches. "No."

"Okay," I say and start to turn around. His quick refusal hurts a little more than it probably should for only having known him a few weeks. "So, see you next—"

His hand on my wrist stops me, but I can't look him in the eye. Embarrassment has my face flaming.

"I just don't think coffee is going to help with your inability to sleep. Maybe water instead?"

"Water?" I finally manage to look up at him, and a little grin plays on my lips at the teasing sparkle in his pretty blue eyes.

"I'd love a glass of water."

Maybe his mouth has suddenly become just as dry as mine.

Chapter 15

Quinten

"I don't think I've ever seen that before," Hayden says, indicating the slice of orange floating in my glass.

We decided on a small diner down the road from the gun range, and I kept my eyes on her headlights the entire drive over, smiling every inch of the way because she asked me out before I could do the same to her.

I hated hearing that she was sticking around the shop because she was scared to go home rather than because she was waiting for me to finish up with the ladies straggling behind after class ended.

"I've been doing it since I was a kid. I have no idea when exactly I started though."

She smiles at me, and man, do I love the look of happiness on her face. It beats the irritation and annoyance I've seen too many times to be comfortable with.

"You make it sound like you're old or something."

"Thirty-five isn't old?" She shakes her head. "But older than you?"

She gasps in mock shock with her hand to her chest. It draws my eyes, but I find her eyes quick enough that I pray she didn't see me look.

"Do I look thirty-five?"

"You don't look a day over—"

"Let me save you the embarrassment. I'm twenty-nine."

"I was going to say thirty-two."

"Jerk," she snaps with humor as she tosses her balled-up straw paper at me.

I chuckle when it flies over my shoulder.

"Well, at least your shooting is better than your throwing aim." Her smile grows. "Tell me about work."

"Work? I'm an accountant. It's pretty boring, but I'm good at it."

"It's not tax season."

Her grin grows wider. "You assuming that accountants don't do anything but taxes is like me thinking you sit around and clean guns all day."

"Who says I don't?" I wrap my hand around my glass of cold water in an effort to prevent myself from reaching across the table and tangling my fingers around hers.

"Do you?"

"Not even close. I'll share some about what I do, but ladies first."

"I work for a firm that subcontracts jobs overseas. I mostly just make sure the amounts are correct for billing and that what's coming in and what's going out are what they should be. See? Boring."

"Overseas jobs? Like local businesses that contract labor for manufacturing."

"Not exactly," she says, and her eyes drop back down to her glass of water. "I can't-I'm under contract—"

"Oh," I say, thinking I understand correctly. "It's government stuff, which means there's a security clearance required."

She gives me a weak smile that confirms what I ask but doesn't verbally verify, which is all the verification that I need.

"A lot of my job is confidential, too."

"Anything you can tell me about?"

"Nothing specific, but I can say I work with some of the best men I've ever met. We each have our own niche of expertise, and sometimes the jobs we're hired for requires several of us to work together. Those jobs are the most thrilling. We travel some, mostly dealing with domestic issues."

"Like cheating spouses?"

I can't help the laughter that bubbles out of my throat. "We've done that in the past, but I mean domestic as in the USA."

"But you do travel some outside of the country?"

"On occasion. Some of the other guys more than me. My skills are usually spent on the phone or through written documentation."

"So you teach different classes?"

"This is my first class to teach. Kit Riggs is our weapons guy, but he had a conflict."

"You didn't want to do it," she says.

"I don't mind it now that it's started." I don't mention that I look forward to Thursday because it's when I've been able to see her. I hate that we only have one class left together, and she didn't seem too thrilled about the idea of me helping her learn how to clean a gun.

"You were very assertive that first class, and then again when you called me." Her back straightens as if thinking back to those first interactions have her getting angry all over again.

"I'll admit that I wasn't exactly thrilled about teaching a class to fourteen women. Fourteen," I repeat for clarification. "Not fifteen. I was given specifics, and if there's anything you'll learn about me is that I tend to be very rigid where rules are concerned."

"Even to the point of throwing two women out of class?"

"I didn't throw you out."

"But you had to know I wouldn't stay if Parker had to leave."

"Because you drove together? She could've easily waited around for you or come back to pick you up. I would've offered to drive you home even." I clamp my mouth closed, feeling like I've said too much, but then her smile changes from one of forced pleasantness to one that's a little slyer, and I can't help but find the pull of her lips a little flirty.

She asked me here, but I can't decide if this is some sort of date. It feels like a date. I want it to be a date, but I'm not sure where her head is at. Maybe she'd rather sit here and talk about work than go home, and if so, that makes me wonder just how much she's downplaying her fear after the break-in at her house.

"And you think I'd get in the truck with a total stranger?"

"I'm just saying you had options, and I think I corrected the issue when I called you the next day."

"You called because you felt bad?"

I clamp my mouth shut.

"Really?" she snaps with a light laugh. "Someone else told you to call me?"

She plops her back against the back of her chair making me realize she was leaning in toward me despite a full two feet of table separating us.

"The guy at work who set up the class firmly suggested that I call you and tell you that you and your friend were welcome back," I explain, not going into detail about why Wren was so adamant about her attending.

"Wow, and here I was softening up to you because I thought you wanted me in class." She's teasing me, but I can still see a flash of embarrassment for making her feel unwelcome that first evening.

"I'm glad you came back, Hayden. It's been nice having you in class."

"As nice as having Gayle? She's missed two classes."

I don't want to think about Gayle right now, but according to Wren when I asked him about her absence last week, he couldn't find anything on her since the Tuesday before. Her credit cards haven't been used. She hasn't been arrested or hospitalized, but telling her that we're tracking the woman from the group opens me up to her possibly asking other questions, and I don't want to have to lie to her. I also know that the truth could possibly make her jump up from the table and never want to see me again. Knowing why she's in class started as a way to ensure we helped the women that need help the most, but now it makes me feel a little dirty.

"Maybe she thinks she learned all she could. It's a beginner's class after all. I'll check with Adam and see if maybe she signed up for a more advanced class."

She smiles, seeming appeased with the lie.

The evening goes on, the two of us making small talk and getting to know one another, but that teasing, flirty smile she threw my way earlier never reappears, and when I walk her to her car, I keep my distance when really I just want to wrap my arms around her and hold her against my chest.

I regret now that she asked me out first.

"So, class on Thursday?"

"I'll see you then," I tell her, opening her car door when she stands and lingers for a few seconds.

Does she want me to kiss her? God, I'd pay money to be able to read her mind for just thirty short seconds.

She gives me a little wave before climbing into her car. Like a fool, I watch her taillights disappear before making my way to my own vehicle.

Chapter 16

Hayden

I've been up for hours when I hear the knock on the door. Not because I'm an early riser, but because I just can't sleep. Despite tossing and turning all night, I knew I couldn't stay in bed all day. It would only throw off my schedule.

I got up just as the sun started peeking through my curtains and plan to stay up all day, and maybe at bedtime, I'll be exhausted enough to get a good night's sleep.

Since it's Saturday, I'm already halfway through my routine of cleaning everything in the house. I swipe a hand over the wet spot on my t-shirt from washing the individual pieces of my coffee maker as I inch toward the door. I creep up to the peephole a little leery of who could be at the door, and gasp when I see Quinten standing on my front porch step. A slow smile crosses his face, and I know that he heard my reaction from the other side.

"C-Can I help you?" I ask through the door as I swipe at my messy hair.

"It's Quinten, Hayden. I found a solution to your problem."

I have no immediate idea of what he's talking about. We spent over an hour chatting at the diner, but I was careful to make sure I didn't complain too much, remembering Parker telling me once that men don't like it when women constantly bitch. I found myself wanting Quinten to like me, to want to spend more time with me. I didn't want to complain all night and chase him away.

"Okay... what problem? And how do you know where I live?"

He steps to the side, somehow knowing I'm once again looking at him through the peephole, and I see another man with him.

"Your address was on the paperwork you filled out for class, and we have a copy of your driver's license, remember? This is Wren Nelson. He's the IT specialist at Blackbridge." The other guy smiles and waves, and I feel ridiculous watching this happen through a tiny hole in my door. "He brought everything you'll need for a security system."

Wren holds up a canvas bag as if he needs to show proof.

"I didn't know you were coming." There's no way I'm letting these men in my house looking the way I do.

"I wanted it to be a surprise," Quinten says. "We can come back another day."

That sounds like an even worse idea.

I flip the deadbolts and tug open the door. My hand immediately goes to the chaotic mop on the top of my head. "I've been cleaning. I'm a mess."

"You look beautiful," he says before clamping his mouth closed.

His friend laughs, wheezing out a rush of air when Quinten elbows him in the stomach. "Nice to meet you, Hayden."

"You as well. Come on in." I stand to the side so they can enter. "I didn't tell you about my problem with getting someone out here because I was hinting that I wanted you to do it."

"He's going to get started," Quinten says, pointing to Wren.

"I brought eight cameras, but this size house may only need six. One on the inside and outside of the front and back doors, one in the kitchen, one in the living room and an external one covering the yard and the driveway. I also have one that's a motion activated doorbell."

"Cameras inside the house? What if I want—" I snap my mouth closed before asking if I want to walk around in just a t-shirt and my panties.

"Pretty standard, but it's your house. Tell me what you want, and I'll do it, but I can set it up to where no one has the ability to view your footage unless you give them permission through your home internet or on the app that you'll have on your phone."

"That's fine," I quickly agree.

"So six?"

"Sure," I answer, my face already growing flushed with my near slipup.

I offer them both something to drink, but they decline. Wren gets to work at the back door first, and Quinten goes to stand in the living room, arms crossed over his chest as he watches the street out in front of the house.

I continue my cleaning, sticking close to the living room, of course, just in case Quinten wants to strike up a conversation. I swear I feel his eyes on me more than once while I'm dusting, but when I glance over, his eyes are still out the window. He looks so serious standing there like a sentry guarding my house, and those thoughts of hiring a bodyguard to stand outside my bedroom once again begin to infiltrate my thoughts, but only after an hour of standing there, he knocks, and I invite him in.

I shake my head to clear the thoughts, dropping the can of cleaning spray in the meantime.

"I'm hungry," Wren says when he comes back into the living room. "Anyone else hungry? I ordered pizza, wings, and breadsticks."

"Hard work putting in a security system?" I ask with a laugh. "I could've made you something to eat."

"You are not cooking him a meal," Quinten interjects.

"Is it against company policy?"

"Oh, we aren't here for wor—"

"How many do you have left?" Quinten snaps. "I'm sure we've interrupted her plans. The sooner we get out of here, the sooner she can get back to her day."

Wren laughs, shakes his head, and turns to leave the room.

I go back to cleaning with a smile on my face. Wren just all but confessed that they aren't here in an official capacity, and that only leaves Quinten making this a personal matter. I can't even describe the thrill I get from that knowledge. I'll pay him of course, but I also feel a little giddy that he even wanted to see me again after yet another awkward wave goodbye.

I end up dusting the same spot more than once while Wren worked and Quinten perched near the front window.

The doorbell rings, but Wren gets it before I can grab my wallet to pay for the food.

"I was going to pay for that," I complain when he walks in carrying three large boxes. "Man, you weren't joking about being hungry. Can I get you two something to drink?"

"Don't worry about it. I didn't pay. Quinten did." The man in question frowns as Wren hands him the stack of boxes. "And I can't stay. I just got a text, and I need to head home."

"So the system—"

"It's done. Q here is pretty proficient with the program. He's going to show you how to operate it after you guys get finished eating and before he leaves."

Wren slaps his friend on the back before turning toward the front door. "It was lovely to meet you, Hayden. See you soon."

We both stare in the direction of the front door long after it closes.

"I think he just set us up," I whisper after several minutes, looking in his direction to try to get a read on how he feels about it.

"Seems that way. I apologize. He's not very subtle."

"You can just show me how to work the system. You don't have to stay to—"

"Do you want me to leave? I've been thinking about it, and now that I'm here, it was seriously rude to just show up and barge into your day."

"I don't want you to leave. I mean, I don't mind eating and then learning about my new security system. Do you take credit cards? I don't have checks and I never keep cash lying around."

"It's just pizza, Hayden. I don't expect you to pay for lunch."

"I meant the security system."

"Oh it's... don't worry about it."

"I have to pay for the system, Quinten. I won't take no for an answer."

"It was free," he rushes out. "Congrats! You were the winner."

"Winner?" I cock my hip and prop a hand there.

"It was in the fine print of the sign up for the shooting class. One person was randomly selected to win a free security system."

"You are full of shit." My smile is wide as I glare at him, so I don't imagine he's getting the full effect I'm trying to display.

"Seriously, but I'm obligated to inform you that the even smaller print says that you're responsible for the monthly service fee, and the app has a onetime purchase fee of five dollars and ninety cents."

"Is that right?"

He nods. "Plus tax. Do you want to eat in the dining room or here in the living room?"

"Here is fine," I tell him with a laugh. "I'll call your office on Monday to get all the legal documentation."

"I'll get it for you. Don't want to add another thing to your list of tasks. Can you grab napkins?"

I shake my head as I leave the room, realizing that his visit is the best thing that ever could've happened to me. I didn't know I was struggling so much until I realized that the last man that was in my house was the person who broke in, and that's assuming it was a male.

Quinten being here has replaced that last image, and I get the feeling that it's going to go a long way in helping me start to heal.

The meal is spent mostly in silence, but unlike when he was standing at the window, he keeps his eyes trained in my direction as we sit down and dole out the food.

"If you grab your phone, we can get the app downloaded," he says after we're both done eating. "I won't eat any of this again. Want me to put it in your fridge?"

"Sure," I tell him just before leaving the room to go grab my phone.

We meet back up in the living room, and he quickly finds the app after I hand him my phone.

"I went ahead and put my number in your contacts in case you have questions after I leave."

He swallows when I smile, and we spend the next half hour going over how the system works and how to pull up video from an earlier time.

Instead of him getting up to leave when it's done, he sticks around, striking up a conversation about my house.

"Do you like living here? It seems like a nice neighborhood."

"I did. It doesn't feel as nice after being broken into, though."

"Criminals don't tend to rob poor people. I showed you that anytime someone activates the motion camera near the front door, your voice will ask them if you can help them. That will deter almost anyone coming from doing something bad. Robbers prefer not to run into homeowners when they're stealing. It increases the chance of them getting caught."

"That makes sense."

My phone rings, and Parker's name flashes across the screen. He stands from the sofa even though I hit the decline button.

"I should get going. There are a few cases at work I need to wrap up."

I stand as well, walking with him toward the door.

"Thank you for doing this for me. Seriously, about the payment, I think—"

His lips are on me, just a slight brushing of his mouth against mine, but when he pulls away too soon, I can't even remember what I was going to say.

"I'm sorry. Shit, I shouldn't have—"

"I liked it," I confess.

Instead of bending down to kiss me again, he gives my hand a quick squeeze and then leaves.

I don't think I quit smiling for the rest of the evening, and when I go to bed that night, I sleep very well with the reenactment of that simple kiss playing over and over in my dreams.

.

Chapter 17

Quinten

"Is that something else you learned with Jude," I tease Hayden.

She bites the corner of her bottom lip as she blinks up at me.

"I don't know what you mean."

"You're counting your breaths as you shoot, and you pull the trigger on every third exhale."

"I didn't realize that's what I was doing."

"You were fully in the zone. It's good to see. You've come a long way."

My eyes stay on her mouth. I had apologized Saturday for kissing her without warning, but more than anything, I regret not kissing her harder, longer, with more intensity. I regret walking away before knowing what her hair feels like tangled around my fist, or what her tiny body feels like pressed against mine.

I nearly groan when she licks her lip before answering. "I've had a great teacher."

"I think it has more to do with you being an excellent student."

"Is that so?"

Her cheeks begin to turn pink when I push a lock of hair off her cheek.

I'm thirty-five damn years old, and this woman makes me feel like a boy with no flirting skills. I swear I'll dig a hole and bury myself if something ridiculous like *aw shucks* slides out of my mouth.

Flirting, I know how to do. I've done it before with a very high rate of success, but picking up a woman in a bar and actually wanting to spend time with someone outside of the bedroom are two very different things. I don't just want to score with Hayden. I want to spend time with her, talk to her more about her life and her childhood. I want to make plans with her and sit on the couch and watch reruns on the television. I want Saturdays filled with plans, and lazy Sundays in our pajamas. Shit, when did I let my mind start making all those plans?

I'd say after that kiss on Saturday, but two weeks ago at the grocery store, I found myself wondering what her favorite ice cream was while I was deciding between yogurt and sherbet.

"Did Parker just decide she's too good for class?"

She frowns, her joyous smile falling from her beautiful face with a speed that would challenge the fastest car on the road. And just like that, I manage to ruin the light flirting I was able to manage.

"She said she had to work."

"Well, I'm glad you've made every one. What do you say to—"

"Mr. Lake, can you help me? I think it's jammed."

Regretfully, I turn away from Hayden and go help one of the other women. I am still teaching a class after all, but in less than an hour, that duty will be over, and I can put all of my focus exactly where I want it to be.

Every second I spend helping the others in class goes too fast. Unlike the time at work that drags so slowly I question the clock on my office wall more than once a day. Being with her in the same room and still being several yards away from her, the time ticks away too quickly. Our time together is coming to an end unless I can find the courage to ask her to go out with me again.

She's had my phone number for the better part of a week, and not once has my cell chimed with a text or a call from her. Maybe I wasn't specific enough in telling her that I wanted her to call just to chat, and that she should feel free to use it at any time, day or night. Stupidly, I specified if there was a problem.

When the women in class begin to trickle out and leave, I'm fairly confident in their abilities to shoot safely. Before today's class started, I gave them information on Adam's class that will help them go from beginner shooters to ones with steady skill. Many of the women signed up for that second class.

I smile when I see Hayden lingering, taking her time to use the ammunition allotted from today's class. Eventually, she's the very last person left in the room, and I walk toward her with confidence, standing to the side until she empties her magazine and sets the gun down. She slides the target back in our direction, and there's proof of her improvement in the tighter clusters of shots on it.

"See? You're doing amazing."

She's beaming when she looks at me.

"Did you sign up for Adam's class?"

She shakes her head. "I'll continue to shoot some after work, but I tend to do better when the room isn't so crowded."

"Understandable. So I was wondering if you'd like to—"

My phone rings, cutting off my words. Pulling the thing from my pocket, I see that it's Wren. I hit decline and look back at her, but before I can start talking, he calls again.

"What?" I snap into the phone.

"The police found Gayle."

"Is she oka—"

"They found her body, Quinten. Deacon wants you back at the office."

My gut sinks. We knew something was wrong, but Wren hadn't been able to find anything on her for close to two weeks.

"Be right there," I snap before ending the call. "I have to go to the office."

"Have a good evening," she says, her voice soft and understanding.

I give her hand a squeeze and leave the room. I'm not going to tell her about Gayle. News like that would only upset her, but as I climb in my truck, I realize I should've said something more. We won't have another class to meet up for, and I doubt she'll use my phone number just to chat.

I make a mental note to text her this evening, apologize for using her information for personal use, and then pray she keeps the communication open, but for right now, I need details on what happened with Gayle, and how we missed being able to help this woman.

***

"My bots weren't set up for that!" Wren is saying when I walk into the room. "I was tracking the same stuff I did to sort the list of sign-ups. And let me remind you, that you weren't happy when you found out I was digging that far into their private lives."

I push through the office door to find the IT guy pacing in front of his computer. It's clear that he's been pulling at his hair, and the tension in the room is so thick even the bird is quiet.

"And no one is saying this is your fault," Deacon says softly. "There's nothing we could've done to prevent this from happening."

"Did we give her a false sense of security?" Wren asks, his eyes finding mine the second I step into the room.

"I can't answer that. She was very gung-ho about shooting. I didn't see it going this way. I figured if anything, she was going to hurt someone else. Can you fill me in on what's going on?"

"Gayle's body was found at a quarry near Columbia, Illinois early this morning. She'd been beaten and then stabbed to death."

"When?"

"Preliminary reports are saying she's been dead over two weeks," Deacon answers.

"So probably since we lost track of her?"

Wren nods. "I should've seen this coming. She's had so many bad relationships. I had to wait until her name was released to even contact the police to give them the info I had because my research wasn't exactly done legally."

Deacon frowns again at his admission. "I'm not pissed because you went looking for information after she didn't show up to class. What grinds my gears is having to find out you were doing it from the Columbia Police. I could've handled the call from them a little better and in a much more professional manner if I was informed. Take a breath, Wren. We've done all we can do. She was already gone before you started looking, and we can't follow these women every second of their lives."

Wren sighs, falling into his office chair so hard the thing rolls across the floor until finally coming to a stop when it bumps into his desk.

I'm informed that the police may be calling me to get information on her demeanor and such from class, and when I go home, I'm so lost in my head with having the same feeling of failure where Gayle is concerned, I don't remember to text Hayden.

Chapter 18

Hayden

"Are we going to talk about the lies you've been telling or not?"

"I don't have a clue what you're talking about." Parker's eyes dart across the room as if she's interested in the framed print of the mountains on my wall. Anyone else might think she's interested in the beauty or wishing for a trip there, but I know she hates the cold, and would choose the beach over snow any day of the week.

"That's how you want to play it? You don't want to tell me what you've been doing that's keeping you so busy that you missed the shooting classes?"

She lifts her wine glass to her lips, and for a second I think she's going to spill.

She shakes her head, an almost imperceptive movement, and her complete silence only makes my suspicions grow even more.

"You've met someone."

"I meet people all the time."

"You're spending time with someone," I clarify. "Who is it? Why aren't you talking about them?"

"I've been working."

I gasp. "You're having an affair with Mr. Williams!"

This gets her attention, her head snapping in my direction. The smile on her face is expected. "You mean seventy-three-year-old Mr. Williams?" She scoffs. "Get real."

"His son then?" She rolls her eyes. "His grandson? Oh! Is he really good looking?"

"I'm not dating anyone from work," she mutters.

"But you are dating someone."

"I don't date."

"I hate to break it to you, but spending time repeatedly with someone is dating."

"I've been working," she repeats, and the tone of her voice tells me it's time to drop the subject.

"Fine, but it always comes out in the wash."

"Speaking of dirty laundry." She smiles wide. "Did you ask Quinten out?"

It's my turn to stare across the room.

"I'll take that pink in your cheeks to mean yes."

"We went for coff—water."

"You went for water? Is that a euphemism for something really dirty?" She clasps her wine glass between her hands, holding it close to her chin as she readjusts her body on the couch to face me. It's easy to see she's fully invested in what I have to say and damn near delirious to listen to me gossip rather than make her own confessions.

"No euphemism. We went to a diner after class and had water. He said it was too late for coffee."

Her eyes narrow. "*He* said? As in *he* didn't want coffee, or he said it was too late for *you* to have coffee?"

"That's a weird look," I say pointing to her face. "Why is your face like that?"

"I'm trying to determine if him telling you what to do is hot or creepy."

I chuckle. "I mentioned not being able to sleep well. I suggested coffee. He suggested water so it wouldn't keep me up since it was already evening."

Her face softens. "That is the sweetest thing. Did you invite him back for a nightcap?"

"No." I drop my eyes.

"And this was two days ago?"

"Last week after class," I correct.

"And this week's class?"

"What about it?"

"Seriously? What happened after this week's class?"

I think back to two nights ago and how quickly he had to leave. I was sure he was going to ask me out or something, but he had to rush off. I was disappointed to say the least.

"He had a work emergency. Why do you keep looking at me like that?"

"There's more to the story, and I'm trying to figure out why you won't talk to me about it."

"That sucks, doesn't it?" I give her a pointed look.

"Working," she mutters. "Now spill."

"He came over last Saturday." I point to the alarm panel on the wall. "He had one of the other guys from his office install the security system."

Her eyes dart to the panel before slowly looking back at me. With each inch of rotation of her head, her smile grows. "He did what the other companies in town were too busy to do?"

I shrug as if it isn't a big deal, but deep down I know it is. "He said a random winner was selected from the group to win a free system. I was the lucky winner."

"Bullshit."

"That's what I said."

"The man is hot for you, Hayden. Don't you see that?"

"He's just doing his job, and I really think he has a savior complex. He told me about his job and how he's responsible for crisis management and stuff."

"Mhmm. Tell me more."

"What's there to tell?"

"The man was in your house, Hayden."

"He had a coworker here with him."

"And they both left at the same time?"

My face flames. Parker is my best friend, and I have no clue why I'm getting embarrassed talking to her about this.

"He kissed me, okay!"

She rolls her lips between her teeth to keep from laughing. "Was it a good kiss?"

"It was just like a brush. No big deal."

"If it wasn't a big deal then why are you as red as a tomato?"

"It's hot in here."

"Is not." She chuckles. "You really like him."

"I'll probably never see him again."

"You know where he works, Hayden. Just call his office."

"I have his cell phone, but I'll never use it, and before you grill me, he gave it to me in case I had an operation question about the security system."

"Do you really believe that? Because I don't see Blackbridge making a habit of giving out personal cell phone numbers."

"It doesn't matter. Classes are over, and I'm just going to chalk it up to a lost opportunity."

"That's absurd. It's the twenty-first century. Call that man up and ask him out on a date."

"No."

"Then fake some sort of security system emergency."

"Absolutely not. He's busy. He works a lot. He said so himself, Parker. I'm not going to lie to him just to be able to see him."

"The man is hot for you. He wasn't able to keep his eyes off you in class. Why do you think I teased you so much about him?"

"Making obscene comments about how his ass looks in jeans, and—"

"He does have a fabulous ass."

"I thought you were going to go after him."

"I was trying to get you to make a move."

"You tried to get me interested in Jude."

Her eyes dart across the room. "Who?"

"His friend?" She gives her head another slight shake, but I get a feeling she remembers exactly who I'm talking about. The question is why is she acting as if she doesn't? "The shy guy from the bar that came that night with Quinten."

"If you say so. I never really wanted to date him. The man is too serious for me. I wanted you to realize you liked him."

"There's a difference between finding someone attractive and liking them."

"Don't I know it," she mutters.

"You know I'm here if you need to talk about anything, right?"

She gives me a smile. "Things are going very well in my life. I've been more worried about you after the break-in than anything else."

Way to drag down the mood.

"Things are okay. I'm sleeping a little better with the new alarm system."

"That's good. Are you—"

Her phone chimes with a text, but she stiffens instead of picking it up.

"Aren't you going to get that?"

"Naw. Nothing important."

"You sure?" Just to test her, I reach for the phone on the coffee table, and like the guilty person she is, she snatches it up before I can activate the screen.

"It's umm—Yep. I've got to go."

"To work?"

"Duty calls."

"It's Saturday."

"No rest for the weary."

"You don't work on Saturdays," I remind her.

"This is a different project."

"Clearly."

She lifts her wine glass to her lips before draining it.

"Are you sure you're okay to drive?"

"Only had one glass, *Mother*. I'll be fine."

"And your boss is okay with you working after consuming alcohol?"

She grins but doesn't answer. She knows I'm on to her.

"See you later!" She waves her hand over her head as she walks out of my house.

I follow immediately, locking the door and turning the alarm system on. I have to tap the screen twice before the thing lights up. Maybe there is a problem with the system that will require Quinten to come over here and look at it.

My phone chirps the activation notice from the kitchen counter, and although I don't feel a hundred percent safe, I didn't lie to Parker when I told her things were better. What I didn't explain is that I've spent so much time obsessing over that kiss and working through fantasies that some nights I forget to be scared.

I wonder how long it will be before the memories of him fade completely.

Chapter 19

Quinten

"You're welcome, Mrs. Humphrey. Thank you for following our advice." I drop the phone back into the cradle and look at Deacon who entered my office while I was on the phone with a client.

"Another happy customer?"

"Always. What's up?" He shrugs. "It's Monday evening. Shouldn't you be home with your very pregnant wife rubbing her feet or building baby furniture?"

"I'll have you know the nursery is completely done, and Anna is with her mother this evening."

"And how much longer does she have?"

"Two months. Well, just a little over two months."

I smile. He doesn't have to tell me something is off. I can feel it swarming around us in the room.

"How long are we going to make small talk before you actually get around to telling me what you came in here to say?"

He gives me a wry smile. "Have plans tonight?"

"Deacon. Come on." I rub both hands over my face feeling tired and antsy all at the same time.

"The class went well. Thirteen graduates, and seven of them signed up for the next level class, Adam said."

I guess that's not bad—thirteen graduates from a class of fifteen. Parker Maxwell, Hayden's friend, missed too many classes, and Gayle—I don't even want to think about her, but I get a sinking feeling that she's the reason he's here.

"Just tell me."

"Gayle was murdered by an ex-lover. The police used all the information Wren dug up, and the man confessed within minutes of them going to his house."

"They caught him. That's good news."

"They can't find any DNA on her body though, and his confession was made while he was stoned out of his mind. They're not sure it will stick because he recanted once he was sober."

"They wear body cams, so they have it recorded."

"He also confessed to being Hitler and being in a long-term relationship with Bella from *Twilight*."

"Shit," I grumble.

"Yeah. So, we'll just have to wait and see. I know you and Wren were looking for Gayle when she went missing, but do you have concerns for any of the other women from the class?"

I look at him unblinking, wondering what I should say.

"Not concerns," I say eventually.

"Okay. Maybe elaborate?"

"I like one of the women that completed the class." He stays silent, waiting me out so I'll speak again. "Hayden Prescott."

"The one you kicked out of class?"

I clench my jaw. "I didn't kick her—you know what, semantics. I've spent a little time with her outside of class."

"I see."

"Are you going to jump my ass for it?"

"Class is over, Quinten. You're free to do as you wish. Do you think she's going to turn into a woman scorned and leave a bad *Yelp* review?"

I huff a laugh until I see that he didn't ask the question with humor.

"Really?"

He shrugs. "BBS is a business like any other. We were trending online for the better part of a month. Hordes of people have contacted us because of that popularity, but there are also people out there that want to see us fail. I'm just wondering if there's going to be backlash if she's unhappy when it ends."

"Ends? It hasn't even begun yet."

"Oh. I assumed... You know what? It doesn't matter. You're a grown man. It's none of my business." He looks down at his watch. "My wife is heading home, so I'm going to get out of here. Have a good night."

"You too," I mutter with a heavy sigh when my office phone rings. I notice it's an internal call. "What?"

"You seem chipper," Wren drawls through the phone. "I need to see you."

He hangs up before I have the chance to tell him he can walk his ass down here. Of course, he doesn't answer his damn phone when I dial him back to do just that.

I wave at Jude, Kit, Finnegan, and Brooks in the breakroom as I walk through.

"Busted, you creep!" is what I'm met with when I open Wren's office door.

I don't even spare the bird a glance, but Wren is typing away like a maniac on his keyboard, and it takes several minutes before he deems me worthy of his attention. I wait like I always do because we all seem to be on Wren's schedule and not our own.

"Look," he says when he finally spins around. He clasps his hands in a steeple and presses his fingers under his chin. "I get the appeal. I really do."

"It's late, Wren. I don't have time for games."

"As I was saying, I get it. I really do, but Whitney was into this shit."

"I have no interest in hearing about the freaky shit you guys are into."

Wren shakes his head. "If you don't stop, you could end up in jail."

I cock an eyebrow at him. I've done nothing to land me in jail, but he's piqued my interest. "Is that so? Please, by all means. Go on."

"I helped because I thought you were genuinely concerned. I wouldn't have gotten involved had I known this is what you had in mind."

"It's just fucking creepy!" the bird squawks.

"When I did it, I only used external cameras."

My blood pressure starts to rise, and not because he's accusing me of something I didn't do. I think I know where this is going, and it's starting to make me very uneasy.

"Spit it out," I hiss.

"If you're accessing the cameras outside to make sure things are okay, that's one thing. Watching her in the privacy of her own home is not only illegal, it's something I never thought you'd—"

"I haven't accessed anything, so you need to start explaining. I assume you're talking about the system you installed at Hayden's house."

"What? You haven't?"

"Wren," I growl in warning. "Of course, I haven't. I don't have the login information for that, and you specifically set it up where she had to approve access."

"I have access, and before you rip my head off, I haven't looked at a single thing. I haven't logged in, but as the admin I could if I wanted to. No one else should have access, and they wouldn't even be able to unless they had control of her Wi-Fi."

"What are you telling me?"

"There's interference in the system I installed. Most people probably wouldn't notice it, but the program runs diagnostics every two days just to make sure things are working properly. There's a mild lag in the reception of data on my end."

I scrub my hand over my face. "Break that down for me. I don't speak nerd."

"Someone else has tapped in. The information my system requests is being channeled through another system. It shouldn't be like that."

"You're telling me someone else is keeping tabs on my—on Hayden Prescott."

"That's the way it's looking. I have diagnostics running, but so far it's only bouncing from tower to tower. Whoever it is, is sophisticated because they're giving my system a run for its money."

"Find them!" I snap before turning around and leaving his office.

I don't bother speaking to any of the guys in the breakroom as I haul ass out of the office. Fear is gripping me, making me wonder how long someone has been keeping tabs on her. It makes the burglary in her otherwise quiet neighborhood even more suspicious.

I feel like a complete asshole, because she voiced her fear of being there, and I chalked it up to that one incident and her living alone.

Is it possible someone is planning to hurt her?

Not on my fucking watch. I speed through every intersection. Somehow karma is on my side because I only hit one red light on the way to her house.

Chapter 20

Hayden

I'm just drifting off to sleep, snuggled deep in my bed, head buried under the covers when a loud banging startles me awake.

Fear grips my chest making it suddenly hard to take full breaths without gasping.

Maybe it was part of a dream, like those times you jolt awake when you fall.

But then the banging happens again.

Regretting that I haven't bought a gun, I grab the only weapon I have in the house—a baseball bat I picked up when the company was thinking about forming a softball team. At Parker's urging, I bought all the necessary supplies, and after the break-in, I pulled this from the back of my closet.

"Hayden! Open the door!"

The familiar voice startles me even more. What in the hell is he doing banging on my door in the middle of the night? He could've called or texted. Hell, he could've done that days ago, and I would've been receptive to the attention. Showing up like this isn't winning him any points as far as I'm concerned.

"Seriously?" I snap when I jerk the door open. It doesn't occur to me that I'm alone and any man has the potential to hurt me, especially ones standing on the stoop with angry, scowling eyes.

I lift the bat even higher, resting the heavy thing on my shoulder.

His eyes soften when he looks from the wood and back to my face. "Really? I teach you how to shoot a gun and you answer the door with a fucking bat? Jesus, Hayden."

"If you're interested in a booty call, you're barking up the wrong tree."

I wonder if I spoke too soon when his hands clasp the top of the doorframe and he leans in closer.

"I need you to pack a bag."

"I'm definitely not leaving my house in the middle of the night."

"It's not up for negotiation. You'll need several days' worth. Go, Hayden."

His boot presses against the door, preventing it from closing when I shove it forward.

Maybe I had him all wrong, put him up on some sort of pedestal, because the man is clearly crazy.

"I want you to come with me."

"Really? I'm just supposed to jump for joy that you show up without calling and I'm supposed to pack a bag in the middle of the night. That's not how it works, Quinten. Please leave."

A part of me, that crazy woman who inwardly craves an adventure, questions why I don't just see where this goes, but I shove her voice down like I always do. Adventure at my age is ridiculous. Wild and crazy is meant to happen in college, and even though I missed out on it then doesn't mean I get to act irresponsibly now.

"There's something wrong with your security system."

That stops me cold, and I pull my hand away from trying to shove the door closed.

"What? Are the cameras broken?"

"There's interference."

"Like static?"

His jaw clenches, and it's clear he knows more and isn't too sure about sharing it.

"I'm not going anywhere with you unless you explain what's going on."

Not feeling like I'm in any danger where this man is concerned, I prop the bat against the wall and cross my arms over my chest. In my head, I'm immoveable, but I know he could pick me up and carry me out of here without getting the least bit winded. I also know he'd never do that. At least I don't think he would.

"Wren was running diagnostics, and he says there's a delay." I noticed the same thing the other night after Parker left and again yesterday and today. "He's trying to find out who it is, but he's certain someone has tapped into your system."

My eyes dart to the tiny camera pointing directly at me from just above his head.

"S-Someone is watching me?"

"It's a possibility. Don't freak out. I'm here and I won't let anything happen to you, but I need you to go pack a bag. Like now, Hayden."

My feet move me toward my bedroom before my brain even has the chance to catch up to what he said.

I'm under surveillance? No, that word is used by police, and I haven't done anything wrong. I'm being stalked?

I think back to all the times the hairs on the back of my neck stood up in the last couple of months. I figured it was fear from the burglary but knowing someone could've actually been watching me instead of my mind going wild makes my skin crawl. I move even faster, not really paying attention to what I'm shoving into my suitcases.

He said to pack for a few days, but I fill the two suitcases I have until they're bulging, praying I managed to get a little of everything.

My hands are shaking uncontrollably by the time I drag my luggage out to Quinten. He's fully in the house with the front door closed, and he's standing in the dark living room once again staring out the front window.

"Is there someone out there?" I whisper.

"Not that I can tell. Are you ready?"

He turns to face me, immediately grabbing the handles of the suitcases.

"Yes," I say as I reach for my purse, phone, and keys on the table. "If I packed anything else, I might as well move out."

He's silent as he leads me out the door, waiting patiently with vigilant eyes as I lock up the house. He opens the passenger door for me and doesn't even laugh when I practically have to jump to get inside his truck because of how big it is. He carries my suitcases around to his side, sliding them in the back seat before climbing inside.

"I need to check my account balances before we find a hotel," I tell him as I log into my banking app. I have savings, but I try very hard not to touch that money.

"You can't go to a hotel," he argues as he backs out of my driveway.

I watch my car and my house as he pulls away, wondering how I'm going to get to work in the morning, and more importantly why did I climb inside without thinking of driving myself first.

"Do you need to call anyone? A friend? Your parents? A boyfriend?"

I look in his direction, my finger hovering over the face identity request on my phone.

"I'll call Parker in the morning. My parents live out of state and do you really think I would've gone on that date with you if I had a boyfriend?"

His face transforms, that irritated scowl he's had since I swung open my front door fading away to be replaced by a smile. "That was a date?"

"You know what I mean, and how are you suddenly calm?"

"Because I have you with me, and I know you're now safe. Do you want to call, Parker?"

"I'm not waking her up, besides this isn't her problem. A hotel is fine."

"I'm not trying to freak you out, Hayden, but someone has had access to your security system, which according to Wren takes some sophistication. If they can do that, then they can probably track your credit card use."

I snap my mouth closed. I didn't even think of that. My hands begin to tremble all over again.

"You'll stay with me."

"The hell I will."

His grin grows. "I have a spare bedroom, and it will only be until we're able to find out what's going on and get to the bottom of it."

"I don't want to put you out, Quinten. Seriously, a hotel—"

"You want to share a hotel room with me? My condo is bigger."

"With you?"

"Yes, with. I haven't told you much about work, and I can't really tell you much now, but I can't be certain that someone isn't watching you because of my work."

"Because you taught a shooting class that I just happened to be in?"

"Because I've been seen in public with you. Because I spent all last Saturday at your house."

"Oh." What else could I say right now? "Your job is that dangerous?"

"We've never had an issue like this before, so I can't be certain. Is there anything going on in your life that would make someone want to watch you twenty-four seven?"

"I'm boring. Until the break-in, I really only left the house for work and when Parker wouldn't stop hounding me, but that was for like one drink and then I went back home."

"You're far from boring, Hayden. Could this be something related to someone you know? Parker, maybe? Is she the only one you associate with?"

My mind goes back to two nights ago and how secretive Parker was being. I think that had to do with a man, not something that would make someone want to interfere in my life.

"She's the only one."

"No big dark secrets?"

I scoff. "No."

"I'll need your house key."

I cock an eyebrow at him, but his eyes are focused on the road.

"Is that right? I've never given a key to a man I haven't been sleeping with."

His jaw flexes, and I have no idea why I even said that. I've never given a key to my place to a man before in my life.

He clears his throat. "I need it so I can send someone over to see if there are any clues as to who tapped into your system. And we left your car because I can't guarantee that it doesn't have a tracking device on it."

My blood runs cold. His words make me realize this situation is just getting worse and worse. Maybe staying with him where he's so certain he can keep me safe isn't a bad idea.

"Okay," I agree.

We drive in silence for a few more minutes before he speaks again.

"Are you hungry?"

"It's two in the morning, Quinten. I should be asleep."

The silence returns.

"So umm…" He clamps his hand on the back of his neck as we slow to a red light, but he doesn't look over at me. "So I can let Wren know, how many people have a key to your place?"

I look out the passenger window so he can't see my smile.

"Parker."

"So the guys that had a key were when you lived—"

"It was an ill-timed joke, Quinten. I've never given a man a key," I explain as I pull my house key off the ring and hold it out to him. "Until now."

He takes the key, his eyes finally meeting mine until they drop down to my lips.

He doesn't know what he's asking by insisting I come stay with him.

Hasn't he ever read a damn book? Forced proximity never ends up being just that. We'll either end up in bed or end up hating each other.

As the light turns green, I'm certain of which one I hope it'll be.

Chapter 21

Quinten

My fingers tap on the steering wheel with no rhythm as we pull into the parking garage at my building. I don't know why I'm nervous for her to be in my space. I'm not a messy guy. Hell, I'm hardly home enough to sleep and shower. Most of my free time is spent at the office.

I've casually dated in the past, but I don't think a woman I was interested in on any level has been in my condo since the first couple of months after moving in, and that was in the condo one floor up from where I am now. No one but the guys from BBS have been inside this new one.

And I'm interested in Hayden on every single level possible.

I frown when Hayden doesn't wait for me to open her door, and busy myself with pulling out her suitcases from the back seat. She meets me in the front of my truck, waiting for me to lead the way.

With it being so late, the elevator is waiting for us, and I'm grateful to get her from out in the open and inside the sanctuary of my personal space. I plug my keycard into the slot that allows access to my floor. As the elevator climbs to the thirteenth floor, we stand quietly. The silence makes me uncomfortable for some reason.

"I was on the fourteenth a couple of months ago," I begin. "But they have been remodeling up there."

"Wow," she says when the elevator doors open to the swanky looking lounge area. "I'm in the wrong line of work."

I grin as she walks further down to take in the view from the end of the hallway.

I jump, the sound of something hitting the door coming from the door next to mine. Of all the damn times I've gotten off the elevator to silence, this shit is going to happen tonight?

"What was that?" Hayden whispers as she walks back and stands beside me.

"That was—"

"You'll fucking take it," Wren hisses from inside his apartment.

Hayden clutches my arm when female cries and gagging sounds come from inside his condo.

"He's hurting her," she gasps as she looks up at me.

Goddamn, this woman is beautiful. I'm not into whatever the hell is going on in the next apartment, but fuck if my dick isn't noticing just how close she is.

"Choke on it!"

And of course Whitney does because we can hear the sounds from our spot in the hallway.

"Maybe we should call the police," Hayden urges.

"It's fine."

"It's not fine. He's hurting her."

"Just listen," I insist.

She tilts her head, brows scrunched together like she can't believe that I'm not breaking down the door to protect the abused woman.

"Yes, please," Whitney moans. "That. Do that again."

A loud smack echoes.

"Again!" she screams. "I'm going to—"

"Oh! Oh God!" Hayden clamps her hand over her mouth and her cheeks flame redder than I've ever seen before.

"Maybe we should go into my place?" I point to the door a few feet down.

She doesn't say a word, but she beats me to the door, unable to look me in the eye.

I chuckle as I unlock the door and shove it open so she can go in first. She scowls at me but doesn't say a word.

"I take it you aren't into stuff like that?"

"No," she answers quickly, and I believe her.

She looks absolutely scandalized.

If she were into getting choked and being bossed around, it might make her being here in my space easier because it would make us incompatible in bed. I never should've asked the question because now I'm picturing her between my sheets, naked and squirming, begging me to stop making her come instead of pleading to let her do just that.

Sadly, I know way too much about Wren's sex life, not only because he talks so openly about it now that he's with Whitney, but also because we share a condo wall.

"Let me show you to the spare room," I tell her, making a mental note to text Wren to tell him to keep it down over there since the spare in my apartment lines up with the master in his.

"Wow," she says again once I turn on the light in the bedroom. "If this is a spare, how big is the master?"

"Technically, this is the master, but I prefer the other room."

Like I said, the couple next door doesn't get much sleep, and when they get going, they're not the most considerate neighbors.

"If the people next door are making too much noise, just let me know."

She reddens again, her eyes looking anywhere but at me. God, if she hears when Puff Daddy gets revved up, I'll be embarrassed for her. The bird is the best hype-man a guy can get, but listening to him squawk pornographic commands while his owners are going at it leaves a lot to be desired.

"Okay," she says softly, but I know she'd never open her mouth to complain. "Do you have guests often?"

"No. I actually need to get you clean sheets. The bed was already made when I moved into this unit a few months ago. No one has ever slept in here."

"I think these will be fine."

"No one has slept in my bed either." Fuck, why did I say that?

"This is a really nice place."

"It is. It's part of the benefits package with Blackbridge. I make decent money, but I'd never be able to afford something like this if the rent wasn't discounted dramatically. Hell, I wouldn't even rent a place like this at full price if I had the money. It's more than I'll ever need. I'm kind of a simple guy." I roll her suitcases in front of the walk-in closet. "If it didn't come furnished, I'd have to offer you my bed and sleep on the couch."

"Well, thank you. Hopefully your friend will be able to find out what's going on, and I won't be in your hair too long. If you want, I can withdraw cash in the morning and use that to get a hotel room."

"It's fine," I rush out. "You're welcome to stay as long as it takes."

She nods, her eyes locking on my chest. The attention makes it a little harder to breathe. I linger, wanting to reach out to her, but I don't.

"Well, I'm going to try to get a few more hours of sleep. I have work at nine in the morning."

I open my mouth to ask her to call in sick, but I know she wouldn't appreciate it. I've already plowed into her life and all but taken over.

"Sleep well. I'll get you to work on time," I tell her before backing out of the room.

I immediately shoot Wren a text telling him to keep the kinky talk to a minimum. They must be at an intermission because he responds back quickly.

Wren: *I was planning to gag her anyway.*

Me: *Well, gag that fucking bird too. I don't want Hayden hearing* him yell choke on Daddy's cock! *I heard enough of that shit last week.*

He sends me a series of crying laughing emojis.

Chapter 22

Hayden

When Quinten mentioned hours ago that the condo was fully furnished, he wasn't joking. I'm grateful for whatever considerate person thought to include a handheld clothing steamer on the list of things to include because I packed in such a rush last night that everything in my suitcases is wrinkled.

The bathroom is also fully stocked, which nearly made me cry when I forced myself out of the bed and realized I didn't get anything from my bathroom. I have no personal hygiene items, nor any makeup. I may be in freshly pressed clothes when I walk out of the bedroom, but I still feel like a bum.

I was both sad and ecstatic when I rifled through the drawers in the bathroom looking for mascara that may have been left behind by an old girlfriend.

"Good morning."

Wow. I know I've said that out loud more than once since he woke me up last night, and I'm grateful for being able to just keep it in my head this time around.

Quinten Lake, first thing in the morning… he's just… everything.

If Parker thought he was hot in jeans, they have nothing on the pajama pants that are riding low on his hips.

My eyes are glued to his bare stomach so long he has to clear his throat to get my attention. It still takes me a couple more seconds before I can lift my eyes.

"I didn't know you'd be up so early. I didn't think to put on a shirt. I'm glad I wore bottoms to bed, or you'd have more than an eyeful right now."

I swallow, thinking the view is pretty fantastic, even better than the sleepy city lights from the hallway outside his condo door. I wouldn't survive walking in here to him in nothing but boxers or completely naked. My heart is having a hard time keeping up right now as it is.

With the beard, I guess I should've considered the possibility of a hairy chest, but wow, just wow. My fingers itch to touch him, to trace the muscles of his torso, circle around his nipples, and then—

"Hayden?" He's grinning when I snap my eyes up to his. "Am I making you uncomfortable? I can go put on—"

"No! I mean. It's your place. Wear as much or as little as you like. I mean—"

"Coffee?" He holds up the half-full pot, saving me from further embarrassment. "I like it when your cheeks turn pink like that."

I duck my head, my fingers pressing to the warmth below my eyes. "I'd love a cup of coffee. Thank you."

"Were you able to get any rest?"

"Not really," I answer honestly. "I couldn't turn my brain off."

"Understandable. Cream? Sugar?"

"Black is fine. Thank you."

His fingers brush mine when he passes me the cup, and either I'm losing my mind or haven't had enough sleep to function properly because a wave of heat runs from the tips of his fingers all the way up my arm. I swear it settles on the tip of my breast, and I nearly moan at the contact.

"You okay?"

"Wonderful," I lie as I lift the cup to my lips and take a tiny sip. "This is delicious."

He laughs, a deep baritone sound rumbling from deep in his chest. "It's Folgers. Simple man, remember? Did you let your friend know where you are?"

"I shot her a text earlier. I can ask her if I can stay at her place."

"I want... until we know what's going on, I'd prefer you to stay here. There's no sense in putting anyone else in danger."

"Okay," I agree quickly.

He turns around to fill his own cup, but I catch the smile on his handsome face before he can hide it fully.

"I was thinking maybe—"

A knock hits his door, but instead of looking surprised, he seems annoyed as he places his cup of coffee back on the counter to go and answer it.

"I apologize in advance," he mutters before opening the door without even looking through the peephole.

A pretty girl with purple hair steps in first, followed by Wren, the guy who installed the security system.

"Hayden, lovely to see you again. This is Whitney, my girlfriend."

Whitney crosses the room offering me her hand. "I want to apologize for last night."

I look from her to Quinten in confusion.

"Wren and Whitney live next door." He angles his head in the direction we heard the noises last night.

My eyes widen, and he rolls his lips inward.

"We get a little out of control every once in a while," Whitney continues.

Quinten scoffs.

"Often. We get a little wild quite often, honestly. We'll keep it down."

Wren coughs.

"We'll try to keep it down."

"I thought you were in the guest bedroom?" Wren says.

"I am," I rush out.

Wren turns to Quinten with a devious look in his eye. "Then why is it a problem?"

"She's in the master, which I use as the spare," Quinten explains, and I feel another rush of heat on my face. "I'm in the spare, which I use as the master."

I just made it sound like I was in his room with him last night, and although I don't hate the idea of that, I don't know these people. They may not care who hears or knows what they're doing in the privacy of their own home, but I'm not one to share information like that with strangers, or anyone for that matter.

"I kind of feel bad the man moved out of the bigger bedroom," Whitney whispers. I look at her in confusion, wondering how they could play a part in him moving. She must notice because she leans in even closer like we've been friends for years. "The masters in these condos share a wall."

"Okay. Well, lovely. It was nice to meet you, but I have to get to work."

"We're really sorry, Hayden. I just wanted to come over and introduce you to my girl so you can see she wasn't being hurt last night," Wren says with much more ease than anyone should have talking about the subject. I'm not a prude, but time and place, fella.

"My butt is still a little sor—"

"You heard the lady," Quinten interrupts. "Thanks for stopping by. Next time, call first so we can pretend to be gone."

Both Wren and Whitney laugh as they leave the condo.

Quinten rests his back against the door with wide eyes. "I'm so fucking sorry."

"You had to switch rooms?" He nods. "That's what you meant by if they're making too much noise?"

"Yeah. They're uh, rambunctious to say the least. I'm sure you deduced that yourself."

"And not shy about it, huh?"

He clears his throat twice as he pushes off the door. "Let me get dressed, and I'll get you to work. Unless you'd like to call in."

He sounds hopeful, and as much as I'd like to stay here and spend time with him, I'm not the type of person to call in unless it's a legitimate emergency. Apparently, in my mind, possibly being stalked after getting my house broken into doesn't fall into that category.

"I need some normalcy," I explain.

I sit at the counter while he gets dressed, trying to keep my mind from wandering to the realization that he had to first strip down before putting more clothes on.

We haven't touched, haven't kissed or even talked about that kiss. It leads me to believe he regretted it and seeing as how he apologized for doing it the second it happened, I shouldn't expect any less. But if that's the case, why is he always staring at my mouth. Why is he going out of his way to make sure I'm safe? Is it his personality? Would he do this for any woman, or does he just feel obligated because there's a chance I'm being watched because of something he's done?

"Ready?" he asks, sweeping into the room, the scent of cologne in the air.

Mouth-watering—that's the best way to describe not only how he looks in jeans and a tight t-shirt, but also the scent of him, the air of power that swarms all around, somehow seeming to wrap me in a cocoon of safety even with him a couple feet away.

"I have travel coffee mugs, if you'd like some to go."

"I have a mug at work but thank you."

I don't know if I imagine it or I'm just hopeful, but I swear I feel the brush of his hand on my lower back when we walk toward the door.

We chat about nothing in particular on the drive to my work after I tell him the address, and I get the feeling he's trying to lighten the mood from the drama that my life has become.

With a quick goodbye and a request to text him when I get off work, I climb out of his truck. The office is quiet when I arrive, and I find it unusual that my boss has two men in his office. They both stare at me when I walk by, one of them closing the door before I make it to my desk. My boss normally doesn't get to work so early, but he's been acting weird for weeks.

I grab another cup of coffee wondering just how many it's going to take to get me through the day and get to work. As the day drags by, I regret not taking Quinten up on his suggestion to just call in.

When the guys leave my boss's office, one stares at me like I've personally offended him, but he doesn't say a word.

Thankfully, the rest of the day goes by without incident. When I text Quinten to let him know I'm leaving soon, he texts back that he's already waiting in the parking garage for me. I don't think I've ever rushed out of the office so fast.

Chapter 23

Quinten

She grins, a smile so small it barely lifts the corner of her mouth when she spots my truck as she exits the office building. I climb out quickly and open the door for her, resisting the urge to help her inside by either touching her waist or her glorious ass. God, the woman brings me to my knees, and I don't think she even realizes it.

"Good day?" I ask when I climb into the cab.

"I'm an accountant. I don't think I've had a good day at work since I started."

I frown, hating that she goes to a job she doesn't love. I have bad days at work as well. I think everyone has, but I couldn't imagine waking up each morning with any level of enthusiasm if I despised where I worked.

"Your car is back at my place. They didn't find a tracker on it, and they didn't find anything at your house. I wish I could tell you that we were closer to figuring out just what the hell is going on, but we aren't."

"Okay," she answers, sounding sullen and a little withdrawn. "I hate that I'm putting you out."

"You're not," I rush to tell her. "It was nice to have someone to chat with this morning."

And the way she looked at me? I was barely able to keep control of my erection, a problem I haven't had since my early twenties.

"Do you have a class tonight?" she asks when I pull up outside the gun range.

"Nope. Just here to pick up a package."

"Do you want me to wait?"

"You can come in. Do you want to shoot today?"

I'm anxious to get her back to my place, but I'm willing to do anything to set her mind more at ease.

She opens her door, climbing down once again before I can help her out, and it's a problem I promise to work on. I want to help her. I want her hand in mine when she climbs down. I want to be able to touch her if only for the briefest of seconds.

I wave at Adam when we walk inside. I called earlier today and made arrangements, so he heads to the back to get my purchase without greeting us first.

Hayden waits at the counter with me, her eyes rolling over all the guns on display that they rent out for the firing lanes.

"Here it is," Adam says when he walks up to us.

He snaps open the hard case, and I watch Hayden for her reaction.

She isn't smiling when she looks up at me. "That thing is tiny. Are you planning to hide it in your boot?"

"It's not for me."

She blinks down at the gun, not catching on.

"It's for you."

"Not me," she says, taking a step away from the counter.

Adam disappears silently, and I'm grateful for the privacy.

"I need you to be armed."

"I'm not ready."

"You are," I assure her.

"You can't buy me a gun, Quinten."

"You won it."

"Don't start that shit with me," she snaps, but that teasing grin is on her face once again.

"You can ask Adam. They randomly pick one winner a month from all the people who rented lanes."

"Another lie! I already 'won' the security system. There's no way I got lucky twice. I bet that's not even a thing."

Thankfully, Adam is nowhere to be found. I point to an announcement on the wall that does in fact explain the drawing held each month. "See? I'm not making this up. It's yours. I want you to carry it in your purse."

I'm glad they don't post the names of the winners on the wall. This little fib wouldn't work out in my favor if they did.

"With the luck I'm having, I should've filled out that survey I got in the mail last month that promised an entry for a new BMW."

"Do you need a new car?" I tease.

She slaps my stomach with the back of her hand. "Would you stop? It's really mine?"

"Yes."

"Would you make fun of me if I told you I'm a little scared to carry it around with me?"

"Remember when I told you that a little fear is a good thing, and firearms should be respected? No, I'm not going to make fun of you. It's healthy and completely sane to feel that way."

"Is it loaded?"

"Of course not. You can't have loaded weapons inside this part of the store. Only employees."

"So, you're not armed right now?"

"They consider me an employee." It's not a huge lie. I kind of work here if you consider BBS renting out the firing range and classroom recently. "We'll get it loaded once we get back home... I mean back to my place."

"Okay." She snaps the lid closed.

"In your purse, Hayden."

"It won't fit in my purse." She looks down at the counter. "Maybe Adam can put it in a bag or something."

"Take it out of the case and put it in your purse. You need to get used to the weight of it."

I watch as her fingers tremble a little as she pulls it from the case, feeling a little bit of pride when she doesn't get that troublesome finger anywhere near the trigger. She's come a long way since she finally decided to take those classes seriously.

"Let's grab some dinner," I say as we leave, not really giving her an option to turn me down. "Do you want to sit down or something quick?"

"Do you have a preference because I just want to eat and veg out? You don't have to change your plans for me. I promise not to snoop through your things back at your condo if you have something else to take care of."

I huff a laugh. "I have nothing to hide, Hayden. Feel free to go through every drawer in the house."

"Even the bedside drawer?" Her eyes widen as she clamps her hand over her mouth. "Can we just pretend I didn't just lose my brain-to-mouth filter?"

"I think something quick is a good idea. Are you thinking burger, pizza, Mexican?"

She allows me to open the door for her. Well, I don't hit the unlock on my key fob until we're both standing near the passenger side, and I have no doubt she'd open the door herself if she could.

"I like opening the door for you," I say as I lean in close. "Let me."

She gives me a quick nod, and I hate that I can't see if she's blushing with her back to me.

"Burgers sound perfect. Maybe some place with those seasoned curly fries?"

"Your wish is my command," I tell her as I crank the truck and back out of the parking lot. "And if you were wondering, I don't have anything weird in my bedside table."

She squeaks, and I chuckle at the sound.

"It's empty except for a pair of reading glasses—I am old after all—and a crossword puzzle book I work on when I can't sleep."

I feel her eyes on me, but I resist looking in her direction as I pull out into traffic. Maybe she got my meaning. I don't have condoms or sex toys, meaning I don't tend to have sex in my own bed. Hell, I don't really have sex, and the last time I did, which was months and months ago, I went to that woman's place. It was closer to the bar I picked her up at.

"What's in your bedside table?"

She chuckles, but it's tinged with that same embarrassment, making it so easy to read on her skin.

"You said I could go through your things. I didn't offer the same." Her tone is teasing, and I wonder if talking about or even hinting at something sexual is taking it a little too far.

"Hayden Prescott, do you have naughty things in your bedside table?"

"Sex is natural," she says, more confidence in her voice than I bet she actually feels. "Of course, I have sex toys. Well, one sex toy."

I scrape at the back of my neck. "Did you bring that with you? I mean, you did want me to make myself scarce tonight."

She snorts. "I didn't even bring my makeup. Do you really think I'd forget that and remember to grab my vibrator?"

"I guess it depends on your priorities. I promise not to interrupt if I hear a little buzzing coming from your room."

She drops her pretty face in to her hands. "I cannot believe I'm having this conversation with you."

"Don't be embarrassed. Sex is natural, remember?"

"You like teasing me, don't you?"

"I like to see you smile, and the blush in your cheeks is my new most favorite thing."

She peeks at me through her fingers. "I'm twenty-nine. I know it's a little crazy that I get embarrassed talking about sex. Well, I don't always. Just with—"

"Men?"

"Just you for some reason."

The conversation is cut off as I pull up to the drive-thru ordering menu, and by the time we get our food, neither of us bring it up again.

She nibbles on fries and groans with every sip of her strawberry milkshake, so that by the time we get back to my building, I'm itching to get my hands on her. I settled for a double with cheese and bacon—hold the onions just in case.

She's playful, quick to smile as we eat in front of the television, but it doesn't take long before she's yawning.

"I'm exhausted," she says when the credits for an episode of *New Girl*—my guilty pleasure—begins rolling across the screen.

"Let me get that," I say as she starts to gather all the trash.

"I'm already inconveniencing you. Let me help."

She disappears into the kitchen, but when I head that way, she's already coming back.

"I think I'm going to go to bed," she says, hiding another yawn behind the back of her hand. "Sorry. The day just snuck up on me."

"It's been a crazy day," I agree, closing some of the distance between the two of us. "Do you have everything you need?"

"I think so."

At this point, we're less than two feet from each other, and I'm barely holding on to the ability to keep my hands to myself, and then like something snaps in my head, I reach for her. My hand is so big compared to her tiny frame, and I can't help but stare down at it.

I lick my lips as she whispers my name.

"Quinten?"

She blinks up at me, and God I want to kiss her. I want to offer my comfortable bed for her to sleep in, my arms to hold her so she won't be scared.

"Goodnight," she says, and I realize I spent so much time wishing, that I may have missed the opportunity to act.

"Let me know if you need anything," I say, regretfully letting my hand fall away.

Next stop, cold shower for one.

Chapter 24

Hayden

Last night after throwing away the trash from dinner was so weird that I got up extra early and ducked out to head to work before Quinten even got up. And I don't mean that I just tiptoed out. I literally put my ear to the door to see if he was up making any noise. I didn't know what I would've done if he had been.

It was awkward as hell because I thought he was going to kiss me, but then he didn't. I would've had to jump to bring his lips to mine, and I figure if he wanted to be kissed, he would've made it possible for me to actually do it. I'm sure I was standing there, head tilted back, lips puckered as I waited, and then it just didn't happen.

First the apology for the first kiss, and then last night? The man is really giving me a complex, but I keep putting myself in the position to be rejected and humiliated.

I found my car keys on the kitchen counter last night, and I saw my car was parked next to the space we pulled into last night, making my getaway super easy this morning.

I'm already regretting getting off work and make a plan to contact Parker at lunch to see if she'll go shoot with me. Avoiding going back to the condo as long as possible is on the top of my priority list.

I don't know how much later Quinten stayed up after me, but I found a note beside my purse this morning with an apology for digging through my things and a warning that he loaded my little gun.

The weight of it on my shoulder this morning on the elevator ride down felt much heavier than the couple of pounds I know it to be. Being armed carries a lot of worry and fear rather than a sense of security.

I let the idea of walking around armed sweep over me the times I went to shoot alone, but I don't feel an ounce of that confidence now that I actually am. I'm more worried about it going off and shooting me in the leg, or someone stealing it and doing something terrible with it.

Once I arrive at the office, I spend fifteen minutes in my car just sitting. I'm way too early to be at work, and I doubt my boss will care if I get there before everyone else. I still wouldn't be able to leave until five. I hate giving my time away for free. I told the truth yesterday when I confessed to Quinten that I didn't like my job.

I don't think a single person there is happy, and if they are, it's because they're new and the job just hasn't sucked the life out of them yet. Accounting is a solid skill to have, and I know I can find work elsewhere, but that also means putting in applications and interviewing, and honestly, the idea of that right now with everything else going on makes me even more exhausted than I already feel. It's just one more thing I'll need to add to my never-ending list.

It took hours for me to fall asleep last night, despite being utterly spent. I blame Quinten and the weirdness of yesterday evening. I can't seem to turn my head off where he's concerned and being in such close proximity to him isn't making things better.

First, he teases me about sex toys, and then he maybe almost kisses me? The man can't seem to make up his mind. I do know that I liked the feel of his hand on my hip, hating that my blouse was tucked in rather than wearing a t-shirt or tank top that gave him the chance to actually feel my skin. It didn't stop the warmth of him though. I felt that heat there long after ending the awkward encounter and walking away.

I squeeze my eyes shut, needing just a moment without my head filled with thoughts of him, but closing my eyes brings snippets of my dreams from last night back to memory. Geez, the bravery I'm able to display in my dreams is nothing like the shy girl who walked away last night when all I wanted to do was climb him like a tree and press my lips to his.

Grumbling, I climb out of my car and head to the elevator that will lead me to my floor, hoping that distracting myself with work will keep my mind from wandering to places it has no business heading. I want to be brave. I want to open my mouth the next time I see him and demand he tell me why he keeps backing away. I want to ask him to his face if he wants to kiss me. If he rejects me then, so be it. At least I'll know where his head is at. At least I'll know where I stand. Not knowing has the power to drive me insane.

As the elevator begins to ascend, my phone chirps, reminding me just how early I am because it's the thirty minute warning alarm I've set to prevent me from being late. I pull it from my purse, silencing the alarm and staring down at the otherwise blank screen. Parker hasn't been as interactive as normal lately, and although I'm concerned for what's going on in her life that she seems insistent on keeping me in the dark about, I have things going on in my life that I haven't been quick to update her on either. It seems we both have our secrets.

Stepping off the elevator, I type out a message to her, begging her to meet me after work.

"Is this her?" a man snaps.

My head jerks up from its attention on my phone to find one of the same guys from earlier in the week glaring at me.

My boss is standing behind his desk, his face drained of color. He looks absolutely terrified, his throat working on a swallow and his eyes darting all over the room.

"She has nothing to do with this," my boss finally manages.

"The hell she doesn't. We don't have Feds breathing down our necks because this operation is working smoothly," the guy snaps, never taking his eyes off me.

"I'm s-so- Who are you?"

"Like you don't know," the guy hisses as he advances on me. "Get your ass in here."

I lift my arms to defend myself, but the guy smiles at the defensive stance. He shakes his head, and I know I look ridiculous. The guy is easily twice my size and I scream out in pain when he clamps a meaty fist around my upper arm before dragging me into Mr. Harrison's office.

"She's the accountant, right?" the guy growls, making my boss nod his head.

"But she doesn't know anything. I did what you asked. I cover those accounts myself. I've been—"

"I'm tired of hearing it, Harrison. You know Mr. Pierce doesn't like delays."

The guy releases me with a shove so hard I nearly fall to the floor. My hip hits the edge of the desk, making me cry out in pain. Hot tears burn the backs of my eyes threatening to fall, but I somehow manage to hold them back.

My phone chirps a text just as it hits the carpet under one of the office chairs, and the angry man's eyes snap to mine.

"Did you call the police?"

"What? No." I'm terrified, but even I know the damn police don't text. "I texted a friend."

My hands are shaking uncontrollably, and my jaw is trembling with fear.

"Is she calling the police?"

"I didn't text her about what was going on. I was texting her before you grabbed me."

I only thought I was scared before, then he pulls out a gun.

"That's not necessary," Mr. Harrison snaps, drawing the attention of the gun-wielding psycho. "She has nothing to do with this. Just let her go."

The guy scoffs, an evil sound that rumbles from his chest, and with the noise, I know I'm not going to make it out of here alive. I have no clue what is going on, but that won't stop this man from killing both of us.

"Ch-check it," I urge. "I wasn't texting the police. I didn't say anything about what's going on here. I-I don't even know what's going on."

"You're digging into things that don't concern you," he snaps, his calm menacing demeanor beginning to turn into rage. Unreasonable men are dangerous, and if this man set out to kill my boss today, I doubt he'll have any trouble upping that body count to two.

I watched crime shows religiously before my house got broken into. I know that my likelihood of getting out of this with only the bruise I can feel forming on my arm is slim. I've seen his face. He's hinted that I know too much already. He's said his boss's name.

"P-Please," I beg. "I don't know anything."

"You know enough," he hisses.

The overhead lights glint off the shiny, silver weapon, making my legs grow weak, threatening to drag me to the floor.

My phone rings under the chair, and instead of getting angrier, the man shoves the chair out of the way until it crashes against the wall. Then his boot comes down, smashing the screen.

I instantly regret sneaking out of Quinten's condo this morning. I'd take a million awkward near-kisses if it meant I didn't have to be here right now.

Chapter 25

Quinten

Waking up hard this morning wasn't surprising, considering how badly I wanted to go into Hayden's room last night and apologize for being a weirdo. Not with how far I let my mind wander last night before rolling over and punching my pillow with regret.

I should've kissed her. I wanted to kiss her. I wanted to press my lips to hers and never come back up for air.

But I didn't want her to feel obligated to kiss me back, and I was afraid that's what would've happened. I insisted she come stay with me until we figure out who and why someone was watching her, and although she didn't put up too much of a fight, I know she isn't exactly comfortable with the entire situation. She's a woman who has been, until recently, living alone and not having to share her space with anyone.

I didn't want her to feel as if I only had her there for my own selfish gains. I also didn't want her to feel obligated to kiss me back because of the situation we found ourselves in.

If I had any doubt where she stood, her sneaking out too early this morning is my answer, and I head into work irritated and bordering on irrational. Part of me insists I give her space, knowing I can't force a woman to want me in the same way I want her. The other part of me wants to pick her little ass up, stare into her eyes, and demand that she be mine.

I get the feeling that possessive attitude isn't going to get me far where Hayden is concerned, but despite needing to give her space, I can't help but call her twice on the way to work. The first call rings several times before going to voicemail. The second call goes directly to voicemail, and I guess that gives me my answer.

I'm agitated, fingers twitching with restless energy when I walk into the office, barely even nodding at Pam, the BBS office manager, on my way through. The usual suspects are in the break area, already gearing up to start their day, but I arrow straight for Wren's office.

"I'd knock!" Jude calls after me, just as my fingers clamp over the doorknob. "He was acting weird this morning. Had that look in his eye."

I hit the door with impatient knuckles and wait for Wren to answer. He grunts out an unintelligible response, and I shove open the door. Thankfully, Wren is fully clothed when I step into his office.

"Hey asshole!" Puff Daddy yells the second I step inside.

I close the door behind me, catching Wren's attention. "Must be serious if you're closing the door." His eyes narrow. "Or you're about to ask me to do something you know the others would have a problem with."

"I want you to check up on Hayden at work."

"The latter then," he mutters, and I grow even more agitated when he just sits there staring at me instead of turning around and working his keyboard magic.

"Wren, I need—"

He holds his hand up. "You already have me digging into her life to try to find out who is stalking her. I've given you the dossier, so I know that you know—"

"I haven't read any of it," I assure him.

I didn't want to know the answers to questions I could ask her in person and learn that stuff from her. I want to get to know the woman through her own confessions, not words I've read from a printed file.

"That may be so, but you know that she works for ViCorp, and they have contracts with government agencies. What you're asking me to do isn't as simple at it would be if she worked for a different accounting firm. They do—"

"Government contracts," I interrupt. "I know, but she left this morning without talking to me, and I have a bad feeling."

"Getting rejected can suck, but that's not enough to hack into her office cameras because she's not interested in you."

"Loser!"

I clench my teeth, reminding myself that Wren will never help me again if I strangle his stupid bird.

"Bring her to Daddy! I can show her a good time!"

I run my tongue over my top teeth and glare at my friend.

"Do you realize what you're asking me to do? I could go to prison. Do you know what happens to computer nerds in prison?"

"Bend over boy! Time to pay your rent!"

He points to the bird. "See! Even he knows."

He must sense my mood when I don't laugh. Any other time, I'd find this entire situation comical, but there isn't an ounce of humor on my face.

"I've always said gut feelings are the only things that keep us alive," he mutters as he turns back to his computer. "You can go grab a cup of coffee or something. This is going to take a while."

"I'll wait," I insist, crossing my arms over my chest and glaring at the back of his head.

"Tell Daddy what hurts, baby girl," Puff says in a voice that oddly sounds a lot like Wren's. "That's it, sweetheart. Drink Daddy's medicine."

Wren shakes his head, eyes still on his computer screens while I glare at the filthy bird.

"What are you teaching him?" I hiss as I watch Puff Daddy strutting up and down his perch.

"He's like a two-year-old repeating shit that he hears."

That's a confession if I've ever heard one.

Jesus, it's always the quiet ones, isn't it?

"What's taking so long?" I hiss after several minutes.

"I'm covering my damned tracks. I'm not going to prison because you can't just call the girl on the phone and tell her how you feel. She's staying at your place. I don't understand why you can't see her there."

"Says the man who stalked Whitney when she went to the gym every day." He scoffs. "Says the man who still watches her on cameras you've put in your own condo."

"She's well aware of those cameras. She agreed to them. I'm not forcing surveillance on her."

"Just, work faster," I grumble.

"What happened last night? What did you do to make her duck out this morning? Was it bad sex? Is it an erectile problem? It's common for men your age, so there's no reason to feel insecure about it. You can overcome that. I found a book online that—"

"We didn't have sex," I snap.

"Obviously. That's the reason I'm recommending the book."

"I don't have problems getting an erection. Fuck, would you just shut up and work? I'm not discussing this with you."

He chuckles as his fingers fly over the keyboard. "There. I'm in, but I can only keep my shield up for a little while. Get your fill, and then I have to shut it down and cover my tracks. Deacon would lose his shit if he knew I was doing this."

"This is her office?"

"According to her taxes, yes. She works as an accountant. This is the accounting floor."

"There's no one there."

He shakes his head as he points to movement in an office doorway. "There."

"I can't see shit. Go to a different camera angle."

"There aren't anymore. They don't deal with actual money like a bank would. This is the only camera on the floor."

"Can you zoom in? Where is that?"

Another screen pulls up to the side. "According to the online blueprints I was able to find, that's her boss's office. Chance Harrison. Do you think she has a thing with her boss? Is that why you wanted me to do this?"

I hadn't actually considered that until he opened his mouth. She told me she doesn't have a boyfriend, but she may not consider an interoffice affair the same way she would a relationship that happens outside of work.

"Is that—fuck, Wren. Is there audio?"

"They don't have audio."

"That guy has a fucking gun. Is she in there?"

"I can only see what you see." The camera shot widens. "There's no one else in the office, but her phone is showing as being at work. Now, the parking garage is under the building, so I can't be sure, but it's possible she's up there right now."

"Being held at gunpoint," I growl.

"I'm already sending a message to the St. Louis Police."

The man disappears from sight, and my stomach sinks. I'm miles away, watching what could end up being the most horrific thing I'll ever witness, and I can't help her. I'm a fixer. It's what I do. I see a situation, and I take steps to make it better.

I'm turning to leave, ready to gather the cavalry when the guy reappears in the camera shot, positioning himself in the open doorway. He's not alone. Hayden is clutched to his side, and although I can't see it with their backs to the camera, I know that fucking gun is pointed at her.

"What has she gotten herself into?" Wren snaps as his fingers work, the other two screens he uses, flashing information and windows moving too fast for me to keep up with.

"I've got to go."

"Police are already on their way, Quinten. There's nothing you can do."

"Like hell," I snap. "She needs me. I can—"

"The fuck?" Wren hisses as we watch the man holding Hayden at gunpoint fall to the ground. "Is that—"

"Blood," I answer. "She fucking shot him."

I disappear out the damn door, ignoring the yells from the guys in the breakroom.

Chapter 26

Hayden

"Oh shit."

The mumbled words don't register in my head even though I hear them.

"This is bad."

I stare down at the bleeding man as I pull my hand from my purse. I didn't know if it would work when I shoved my hand in there and pulled the trigger, but the growing red stain on his shirt is enough of an answer.

He's not dead, he's gasping for air, hands shaking as he tries to press a finger to his wound. My first thought is to make sure he can't hurt me. I kick the gun he was holding further away, but telling from the look in his eyes, the man is no longer concerned about threatening either one of us.

His eyes plead with mine, but before I can drop to my knees and help him, there's a rush of activity outside Chance's office.

"Hands up!" an officer yells as he closes the distance between me and the elevator on the far side of the office.

For the second time today, I have a gun pointed at me, and before I can open my mouth to explain, I'm shoved to the ground and handcuffed.

I knew carrying a gun was a bad idea. I don't know that I would change a single thing that just happened, because the guy lying on the floor bleeding was growing increasingly agitated, and I knew it was minutes if not seconds before he pulled the trigger to get my boss to comply.

I have no idea what Chance got himself tangled up in, but from the looks of the situation, it turned bad very quickly.

"For your safety," a police officer says as he helps me to my feet, "I'm going to sit you over here until we can get to the bottom of what's going on. Do you know who that man is?"

I shake my head as he points to the guy who has several officers and a paramedic kneeling down over him.

"Who shot him?"

"I d-did," I stammer.

"Where's the weapon?"

"In there," I tell him, angling my head to the purse still on the floor in my boss's office.

"Sit tight," he says before crossing the room.

I watch as people shuffle around the office, too many people coming and going to keep track of everything.

Chance is handcuffed and sat in a coworker's office chair on the far side of the area near the conference room, and he looks devastated. His head his hanging between his shoulders. As if he can feel my eyes on him, he lifts his gaze to mine.

I don't see sympathy or remorse in his dark eyes. If anything, he's pissed, his glare saying more than words. He blames me for what happened. If his hands weren't handcuffed behind his back, his fingers would be pointing in my direction, and it makes me wonder how much trouble he's going to be in, not only from the police, but from whoever this Mr. Pierce is that the bleeding guy mentioned earlier.

I have no idea what he's done or why he would be in so much trouble that a guy with a gun showed up to the office today, but I can tell that if there's any way for my boss to blame me for what happened, he's going to do it. He may have confessed I had nothing to do with it when I first walked into the situation, but now that his neck is on the line, there's no way he's going to confess and let the police know that I'm just an accountant who was too chicken to see Quinten, so I came to work early and ended up in the middle of a shitshow.

Chance's eyes are still boring holes into me when a man in a suit lifts him to standing and drags him away.

My skin crawls as scenario after scenario rushes through my head. I know this is a wrong place, wrong time situation, but I shot a man. Both of them could team up against me and say I was the one who went apeshit in the office. I brought a gun to work and lost my mind on my boss and his business associate while they were having an early morning meeting.

My mind is wild with conspiracy theories and how my life is going to be ruined when familiar eyes come level with mine.

Tears burn my eyes. Emotions clog my throat, and if I didn't have steel cutting into my wrists from behind, I'd wrap them around Quinten's neck and never let go.

"Hey," he says, his hand cupping my jaw, thumb swiping away tears that have finally begun to fall. "You okay?"

"I'm going to go to prison," I whimper.

"Are you a criminal?"

I shake my head.

"Then you aren't going to prison." He looks over his shoulder. "Franklin, get these fucking cuffs off my girl."

I shake my head at the belligerence in his tone, not wanting him to cause any more trouble than I'm already in, but I watch in awe as one of the guys in a suit snaps his head in our direction.

"Fuck, Lake. Sorry, man. There's a lot going on. I forgot she was over here."

Franklin, a man wearing a black jacket with *FBI* emblazoned on the back, heads in our direction, helping me to my feet before unlocking my wrists from the cuffs.

My shoulders scream in pain as my arms fall forward, my fingers automatically touching the swollen areas around my wrists.

"He was," I begin, my words coming out as sobs. "H-he—"

"Shh," Quinten says as he pulls me against him.

My head rests between his pecs, and I try to focus on the sure pounding of his heart to calm down, but there's so much going on I don't know that I'll ever feel normal again.

His fingers sweep through my hair, his voice low and unintelligible as he speaks to those around him.

His voice grows more growly, making me lift my head from his chest.

"Tomorrow," he snaps.

"It's best to get a statement right after an incident, Lake. You know that as well as I do."

"Do you really think she's going to forget being held at fucking gunpoint by a psycho?"

"Before noon," the man says with irritation in his voice.

"Let's get you out of here."

I stumble a little as he turns me around, and I glare at him when he bends to lift me.

"I can walk," I hiss.

The morning's events have already left me feeling helpless. I'll be damned if this man carries me out of the office like a damned baby. Instead, he takes my hand in his, fingers holding just a little too tight, but I don't complain.

The elevator opens, and we step to the side as even more police and federal agents step into the area. Quinten nods before urging me into the car.

"They're not going to take me to jail?" I whisper once the doors close us alone inside.

"No, Hayden. You're not going to go to jail." His words are gruff and distant, and I can't help but feel like what I've done has somehow changed his opinion of me.

Chapter 27

Quinten

I'm thrumming with unspent energy as I guide Hayden to my truck.

"They have my purse, my ID, my car keys," she mutters almost as if she's speaking her thoughts out loud rather than having any real concern for her belongings.

"We'll get them back," I assure her as we step up to my truck.

I don't hesitate lifting her to the seat, even though she made it clear back at her office that she would flay me open if I lifted her in front of everyone.

"I need my keys to get into my house," she says absently when I climb behind the wheel.

"You can't go home."

All of the danger hasn't passed, and fuck if I'm able to let her out of my sight just yet.

"He didn't say it, but I'm pretty sure the man I sh-shot was the one who broke into my house."

I squeeze her hand across the console, but she keeps her eyes focused out the passenger window.

"The guy you shot was a middleman for a crime family. He's only a small piece of the puzzle. Chance Harrison was into some pretty shady shit, and until the guys on the upper tier of that family are arrested, I need you with me."

She nods in agreement, but I know her lack of argument has more to do with the crash of adrenaline more than anything else. Or she's more scared now than she's ever been, and that makes me want to go back to her office and kick the shot man in the head. She's had enough damn trauma, and I don't know if it helps to know that what happened today and the break-in at her house are related, but it's too much for any one person to handle. I don't expect her to be able to process much of anything today.

She doesn't budge when I pull up to my parking spot, and she's still distracted when I open the passenger door.

"Hayden?" Her eyes find me, and she looks devastated and gorgeous. "Let me carry you?"

She gives me a slight nod, and I don't give her a second to change her mind before she's in my arms and cradled against my chest.

She tucks her face into my neck, and I find myself walking slower to the elevator than I normally would, if only to drag out the contact a little longer. The sound of her breathing fills my ears on the way up to my condo, and I manage to only shift her a little to unlock my door.

I don't know if she realizes it or not, but she's got blood on her clothes from the incident. I carry her directly to the bathroom in her room, standing silently until she pulls her head back.

"I figure you want a shower," I whisper.

When her eyes fall to my mouth, my body instantly responds to the attention, and I'm helpless to think things through when she inches her mouth forward, pressing her lips to mine.

My eyes flutter closed as a harsh intake of air echoes around the room.

When she teases the slit between my lips, I open to her command, throbbing to the point of pain when her tongue swipes across mine. I hold her tighter, clinging to her like a lifeline as her fingers dig into the back of my neck.

The soft kiss turns feral in a flash, and I angle my head to taste her deeper, needing to live in this moment. The fear I felt, completely helpless, watching what was happening in her office was enough to make me crazy. Having her in my arms, especially if she wants it as much as I do, isn't something I'm going to let go of any time soon.

Releasing my neck, her fingers pull at my shirt, and although I know she's probably in shock and working through the last burst of adrenaline, I place her on the bathroom counter, stepping back only far enough to pull my shirt over my head.

With reverence, her hands trace over my shoulders and down my chest. My eyes flutter closed as her fingers trace the muscle definition on my chest.

"I wanted to do this the first time I saw you shirtless yesterday morning."

"Hayden," I whisper as her eyes leave my chest and float back up to mine.

I press my lips to hers again, my own hands working open the buttons on her blouse before searching blindly for the zipper on her slacks.

I want her, but going too far could lead to regret, could make her second guess what she feels for me if done during such a traumatic time in her life.

She doesn't fight me when I strip her down, revealing every milky inch of her skin, and I nearly groan when her legs fall open a few more inches when I step back to kick off my boots and jeans. I discard my socks, leaving my boxers on, and my cock pulses with need when her eyes drop there.

"Shower," I manage before turning around and turning the water on.

I lift a hand to help her off the counter, but she reaches for me once again, pulling me right back against her, our mouths finding each other.

I lift her from the counter, hands gripping her ass and keeping her a few inches shy of my dick. Kissing is one thing, but rutting against her while she's upset and looking for an escape isn't something I'll be able to handle the consequences of.

She gasps when the water meets her bare skin as if she was so tangled up in the kiss, she didn't even realize I was moving her.

"Let me wash you," I say against her lips, and her head dips, giving me permission.

I make sure she's steady on her feet before turning for the bodywash. Using the loofah doesn't even cross my mind because I've wanted my fingers on her skin for weeks, and despite all of my chivalry, I'm clearly not as strong as I'd like to think.

She tilts her head, neck exposed when I spread soapy hands on her shoulder. I want to keep this shower as economical as possible, but washing her stomach tests my resolve. Her nipples, like tiny pink erasers, point to me, and I've never wanted something in my mouth as much as I do those hardened tips.

I have to look away, washing her body inch by inch, hands skating over her thighs and legs, barely brushing the gap between her thighs, and I try to ignore the moans and grunts of pleasure escaping her parted lips.

By the time I get her rinsed and wrapped in a towel, I feel like I've summited Mt. Everest without taking a single breath. My chest is constricted and begging for relief. My cock, still trapped in soaking wet boxer briefs, outlines my need for her, pulsing with my own raging heartbeat.

After leaving the bathroom, I manage to get one of her shirts over her head, groaning once again when I realize it doesn't cover her but an inch past her belly button.

"These too," I whisper, pulling a pair of sleep shorts from the unzipped suitcase in the closet.

Her tiny hands rest on my shoulders as she lifts one leg and then the next and I watch with rapt attention as I pull them up her thighs, my mouth watering for a taste of her skin before it disappears behind the fabric.

"Bed," I grunt, letting her step back. "I'll be right back."

I disappear out of the room, hauling ass back to my own so I can towel off and put some clothes on. I need about a dozen layers between us if I have any hope of surviving this situation.

I pull on a pair of sweats, finding her still standing in the same spot I left her in as I reenter the room.

"Come on," I tell her as I grab her hand and guide her to the bed.

"Stay with me," she whispers as she moves to the middle.

"It would take the National Guard to get me out of this room right now." I climb in beside her, automatically reaching and pulling her to my chest the second I get settled.

Her fingers tease the hair on my chest as her breaths float over my skin.

My cock is hard, but she's touching me so that's not surprising. I ignore the damn thing and hold her closer.

Watching what happened today as it unfolded would stress me out no matter who was on the other end of the video stream, but knowing it was Hayden terrified me. I knew then that I could never lose this woman. This is the first time she's ever been in my arms, and I can't see another day of going without this.

As her breaths even out to mere puffs, I can't help but feel like I'm going to lose her anyway.

Chapter 28

Hayden

I snuggle deeper into the warm arms holding me. I have enough wherewithal to know where I am and who is holding me, but that doesn't stop the thrill from rushing over every inch of my body.

I was so frightened earlier when everything unfolded, but the relief I felt when Quinten showed up was indescribable. How can a man I've only known for a handful of weeks be able to calm me as much as he did?

Was it just the sense of familiarity in a chaotic situation?

I know the answer before my brain can really formulate the question.

I care about this man, and after he didn't back away from my kiss earlier, I discovered that he cares about me on some level. The heat in that kiss was something I never felt before, and it wasn't a placating kiss, one he felt obligated to return because of my current situation. The man wanted me, yet he still held back. He could've had me. I all but offered myself to him, and he kept his distance.

I've never found words so difficult before in my life, and I think it has more to do with being unsure of the answer whereas I usually know what someone is going to say before I open my mouth to ask.

I can't keep living life like this. Today made me realize that I need to take chances because it could all be gone in the blink of an eye.

Maybe it's the way I feel for him or maybe because I've had my eyes opened and I'm realizing I just want to live life, but I don't let fear hold me back when I push against his chest to look down at him.

He's not asleep, but I could tell by his breathing when I woke up that he wasn't.

"Hey," he whispers as his fingers push my hair off my face. "Feeling better?"

The lids of his eyes are lowered, and I can tell he's struggling not to look down at my mouth. My body heats with need, but I still find myself getting shy.

I'm not a virgin, but all other sexual situations I've been in, the man has always been the one to make the first move. I know he wants me, but he seems reluctant to express that.

"Better," I answer as I press my face back into his shoulder.

Maybe words aren't what we need right now.

My hand shakes as my fingers start to roam over his chest. The rhythm of his breath changes as they drift lower, and I smile against his skin when his stomach muscles ripple under my touch.

"That feels so good," he says, his words a rumble under my ear as his arm around my back squeezes me a little tighter.

My soft touch grows bolder as I trace a circle around his navel. He pulls in a sharp intake of air when I tease the top of his sweats. The gray fabric does nothing to hide his arousal, and if I ever doubted his attraction to me, I don't now.

I hold my breath, biting my lower lip between my teeth as I outline his length as far down as my short arm can reach.

I squeal, a smile wide on my face when one second, I'm teasing him and the next, I'm flat on my back, hands pinned beside my head as he settles over me.

"Do you know what door you're opening?"

I nod, hoping we're on the same page.

His mouth finds mine on a growl, and this kiss is nothing like the one we shared in the bathroom earlier. He's not as calm, not as controlled, and I freaking love it. I love that he is losing himself right now because I want nothing short of the real him.

My hips roll, but my movement is limited by the pressure of his body. We groan at the same time, the contact just enough to drive both of us crazy.

"I want to be inside of you," he whispers against my mouth.

I nod enthusiastically. "I want that, too."

"We can't," he says as he pulls his body back from mine.

Like I've been hit in the face with freezing rain, my eyes instantly begin to water. I have to look away from him, wiggling my hands so he knows to back off.

"No," he says, his nose tracing down the side of my face. "Don't think for a second I'm putting an end to this because I want to. Do you have condoms?"

I shake my head.

"I don't either. Can I fuck you raw?"

I must take too long to answer because his head pulls back, a look of pleading on his face. God, I've never wanted to take a risk so bad in my life.

"I'm not on birth control," I confess.

His hips jolt as if the news turns him on even more. Oh God, is he one of those guys that's going to talk about coming inside of me and getting me pregnant? Would I be able to tell him now isn't the best time in my life to do something wild like that? Why do I want to know what he feels like when he orgasms deep inside of me?

I blame the trauma from the day for these racing thoughts.

"Wren," he snaps.

"What?"

"Wren has condoms."

"Whitney isn't on birth control?"

"I'm sure she is, but they play—they have a weird dynamic. Well, not weird, but it's different than—"

"Were you going to get condoms or were we going to have a politically correct conversation about your friends' kinks?"

His smile is radiant as he looks down at me, and I'm hot all over again at the sight of his kiss-swollen lips. Yep, this man absolutely does it for me.

With a skilled roll, he jumps off the bed. "Don't go anywhere."

I chuckle as he runs out of the room. Knowing what's going to happen and not wanting to waste a second, I strip to my skin while he's gone, only for him to return while I'm struggling to get my shirt over my head.

"Unwrapping my present?"

I whip the shirt over my head to find him standing in the doorway with a bruising grip on his cock over his sweats. Just the indication of his size, still hidden behind fabric, makes me force down a lump in my throat.

"Did he have any?"

I'm not entirely comfortable with Wren getting involved in our bedroom business, but this is an emergency.

"I texted," he says, holding up his cell phone. "I'm waiting to hear back."

I frown, making him laugh. "There is so much more we can do while we wait."

I throw my shirt to the floor, ready and waiting for him to suggest getting on my knees, but then the man crosses the room and crawls up the bed from the end, gripping my ankles and spreading my legs.

His mouth is hovering over the apex of my thighs as his heated eyes peer up at me.

"I normally don't have time to date, but I wanted you to know that this isn't that."

I nod because what else can a woman do when a man sets her on fire then puts his tongue within inches of the most sensitive part of her body?

He doesn't want a relationship? Fine, I can handle that, but I'll do it tomorrow after—fingers crossed—a couple of glorious orgasms.

I forget all about his words and spend the next fifteen minutes trying to remember how to breathe while he licks, nips and sucks on my clit until I have to beg him to stop. I'm boneless, shaking like I'm freezing, and willing to offer him anything I own if he pulls back for a few minutes to let me get my wits back.

He's relentless, using his tongue and teeth in an expert way I've never experienced, then the tip of one finger joins the party and my back hurts from the muscles contractions.

The doorbell rings, and it sounds like the tinkle of a distant alarm, one that barely registers in my head, but he doesn't stop until I'm seizing around that one prying digit and pulsing against his mouth.

His lips are cherry-red and swollen, beard damp with me when he pulls back. His eyes light up with devious intent as he glances from my face to my sex.

"Hold that thought," he insists as he backs out of the room.

I couldn't walk right now if I wanted to escape and getting away is the very last thought on my mind. If the man is that skilled with his mouth, what kind of pleasure could he wring from my body with other parts of his anatomy?

I watch as he reenters the room, a small basket in his hands. I open my mouth to ask him what he's carrying, but then he drops his sweats, a single condom in his hand, and words fail me.

He is absolute perfection, the tip of his glorious erection weeping.

"Fuck, baby, you're really good for my ego, the way you're watching me."

Sure fingers roll the latex down his length, and I'm entranced like a cobra following the tip of a flute as I rise out of a wicker basket. His cock jolts, bouncing with each step as he makes his way across the room to me, but he doesn't settle between my legs like I expect him to.

He lifts me like I weigh nothing, settling me on his thighs, his glorious cock hard and hot between us.

"I'm pretty big," he says as his lips find my shoulder.

"I noticed."

"You're really tiny. Oh, fuck," he groans when I wrap both of my hands around his cock. His hips jolt up, nearly knocking me off his lap. "I don't want to hurt you, so I need you to control this."

"I don't mind doing some of the work. You've done so much already," I whisper as I dip my mouth to his, tasting myself on his lips.

His hands once again lift me under my ass, much the same way he did when he carried me into the shower earlier, only this time he doesn't keep the distance between us. My clit scrapes up the length of him, and as eager as I am to come again, I want it to be with him inside of me rather than the tip of his cock rubbing against me that way.

He groans into my mouth when I reach down to line him up, his fingers curling into my flesh when I lower myself down slightly.

"Damn it, Hayden."

He pulls back, his eyes staring into mine as I drop lower. My mouth falls open as I try to adjust to the stretch his body is demanding of mine, and I can't help but look down, pressing my forehead to his as I watch him disappear inside of me.

"Squeezing me so fucking tight, baby," he hisses. "Jesus, that feels amazing."

I whimper with need as I circle my hips, wanting him completely inside of me but unsure if it's even physically possible.

I lift a few inches before trying again, realizing that I won't have to do much more to climax. He's hitting every spot inside of me, some I never knew existed, and it makes my legs shake.

"Can you take more?" he pants. "Don't want to hurt you."

"F-feels s-so good," I stammer. "M-more."

"Like this," he urges, his hands moving my pelvis forward. "Lean back."

The action opens me up just a little more, but we both watch, eyes glued to where we're connected as I slide all the way down.

His head snaps up, eyes trained on mine as he lifts me with the shear strength in his forearms before letting me slowly glide back down the full length of him.

My lips part on a moan, hands clamped on his shoulders as my legs begin to shake.

"Yes," he whispers. "It's mine. Give it to me."

"Quinten," I hiss when my body seizes up a split second before exploding.

His hips jerk, cock stabbing into me, and I love it. My eyes flutter closed before I can stop them, so I miss the sight of his handsome face when he orgasms but the rumbled groan echoes around the room. He fucks me through his orgasm, cock kicking inside of me countless times.

When it's over, I crash against his chest, more exhausted than I was when I laid down right after our shower. The next thing I remember is the lulling sound of his heart beating against my ear.

Chapter 29

Quinten

Although it's something that rarely happens, waking up with a woman in my arms doesn't feel the least amount out of place. Knowing it's Hayden's breath skating across my skin when my eyes flutter open fills me with a sense of rightness so perfect, I'm hesitant to move in fear that it could end.

But my body is thrumming, cock hard and ready for more. I waiver between climbing out of bed and making us something to eat, stroking myself hoping that she'll wake up and take over, and crawling down her body and sucking on her clit until she wakes up.

All three are viable options, but then her stomach rumbles in her sleep, making me realize we've been in bed for hours. The sun has set, indicating the day is ending, and she hasn't eaten. My own stomach barks out a protest when her fingers flex against my chest and option one seems much less viable.

I'm trembling with unspent energy despite the restful nap I got this afternoon with her on my chest as I slowly extricate myself from the bed without waking her. I came close to losing her this morning, the threat of one man with a gun having the power to shatter my entire world, and I have nowhere to focus that energy. I grab my sweats from the floor and tug them up my thighs, the entire time keeping my eyes on her sleeping form as if she'll disappear if I look away.

My stomach grumbles again, loud enough that I'm afraid it's going to wake her, and that's the only thing that gets me moving toward the kitchen. I snack on prepackaged grapes as I bend my head, looking in the fridge when I feel the air around me shift.

I turn, my heart ramping up to twice the speed when I see her standing on the other side of the kitchen, her body swallowed up in the shirt I took off and threw on the bathroom floor earlier before our shower.

She holds it to her nose, hiding a smile that's still clear in the sparkle in her eyes.

"Hey," I whisper. "How do you feel?"

"A little sore," she confesses, her face still hidden behind the shirt she's wearing.

I swallow thickly, my cock, and in all honesty, every other part of me, liking that she can still feel where I've been even several hours later.

I want to beat my chest like a savage when she gets closer, each step tentative, indicating just how tender she actually is. I feel like a wild animal, taking pride in the echo of my cock still on her sensitive skin.

She moves before I can fully reach for her, and I figure now isn't the best time to ask her if she wants me to kiss it and make it better.

"I'm umm—" I clear my throat. "I figured you'd be hungry. I'm figuring out something to eat. Do you have any preferences?"

"Maybe just something light. I get the feeling I'm not going to stay awake for long."

"A sandwich?" I offer.

"Do you have cereal?"

I close the fridge door and open the cabinet. "I have Raisin Bran."

"That sounds perfect." We reach for the same cabinet where I keep the bowls, but she shies away a little, making me wonder what's going on in her head.

Is she still traumatized from that man grabbing her and threatening her life with a gun pointed at her? Of course, she is. A nap and amazing sex doesn't make that go away suddenly.

"Here," I say, offering her the bowl and taking a step back before grabbing the milk out of the fridge.

My stomach is twisting, turning in knots, and I want to ask her how she's really doing, but the way she's carrying herself indicates she doesn't want to talk about it.

Once she pours milk into her bowl and steps away, I move to make my own bowl even though I no longer feel like eating.

I want to claim her, to sweep her up in my arms and vow to protect her for eternity, but at the same time I don't want to push her away either. I hate that I don't know how to act or know what to say to her to make it all better. I can't vow that she's safe. I don't know who else is involved with that man back at her office, but I know enough about criminals to know the head guy seldomly shows up to confront the low man on the totem pole himself in person. Doing so isn't good business, especially when shit can go sideways like it did this morning.

I hang my head, arms locked on the counter when she disappears from the room, only taking small comfort when I hear the television in the living room come to life. At least she isn't disappearing and insisting on being alone.

I quickly make my bowl of cereal, returning the box to the cabinet and the milk to the fridge before grabbing a spoon and following after her. She's sitting at the far end of the couch, eyes trained on the television instead of looking at me when I enter the room.

God, if she regrets what we did, I don't know that I'd be able to live with myself. I checked in with her when she touched my cock that first time to make sure she knew what she was doing. At the time, she seemed so sure, as if she wanted to continue down that path we were walking, but now she seems distant and unsure.

"I'll make sure to get you to the police station in the morning since your car isn't here. I bet they'll have your purse there as well."

She nods as she circles her spoon in her bowl. I haven't seen her take a bite yet, and if I had to guess, I'd say she's hungry but doesn't feel like eating. I imagine her stomach is in knots.

"You're going to be fine. You won't be in trouble," I assure her.

"I shot a man."

"A man that was holding you at gunpoint," I remind her. "It was self-defense."

She looks at me for a brief moment before turning her eyes back to the television.

"What we did earlier—"

"I just want to eat and go back to bed."

I nod, not willing to press the topic past what she's comfortable with.

My cereal tastes like sawdust in my mouth as characters on the television laugh and joke about stupid shit. I can't help but feel like that comedy has no place in our situation right now. She doesn't change the channel and pick another show as the sitcom plays out. It's like she's here in body, but her mind is on a totally different plane of existence.

All too soon, she stands from the sofa. "I think I'm going to go to bed."

I follow her to the kitchen, placing a hand on her back as she stands at the sink washing her cereal bowl. She looks up at me with a soft smile, but it doesn't even get close to reaching her eyes. She doesn't turn to me or lean against me as she shuts the water off, drying her hands on a dish towel.

"Goodnight," she whispers, and I stand in the middle of my kitchen, listening to the guest bedroom door close with a soft snick.

After only a couple of hours in her bed, my room feels foreign to me. Her scent isn't in here. The shape of her tiny body isn't on my bed. I hate her being so close, yet completely unreachable.

I strip naked and climb in my own bed, punching at my pillow in anger as I turn to my side. Picking up women isn't hard for me, but I have no clue when it comes to the one I can see myself keeping forever.

Getting shot down by a woman in a bar just means it wasn't my night and I could try again there or go to another place to risk my luck.

Losing Hayden isn't an option, but it's nearly impossible for me to keep my distance from the only woman I can see myself having a real future with. I'm so out of my element it isn't even funny.

Chapter 30

Hayden

My body is trembling, the gunshot echoing in my head as I clutch my own stomach in pain. My heart pounds in my ears, silencing every other sound.

The touch to my arm makes me scream, but when I spin my head around, it isn't a man with a gun but Quinten looking down at me from the side of the bed with pain in his eyes.

"Hayden? Baby, it was bad dream."

I inch away from him, struggling to separate the two realities. The dream was so real, the pain I felt enough to take my breath away, and yet it wasn't. It was all in my head even though I can feel the burn from the bullet still in my gut.

"He shot me," I sob. "He pulled the trigger before I could."

"A nightmare. Come here."

I don't hesitate crawling in his lap like a child when he urges me forward. I wrap my arms around his neck wondering why he was gone in the first place. Then I remember that I came in here alone. Everything felt so awkward when I saw him in the kitchen earlier.

I don't date, he told me before rocking my world with his mouth then his cock. I went into that situation knowing nothing would come of it, and here I am putting him in another situation where he's forced to act as my guardian when it's something he doesn't want.

He holds me tighter, his lips against the top of my head, as my tears begin to fall.

"I've got you, Hayden. You're safe here. Just relax."

He rocks slightly, the motion both soothing and destabilizing. I should be stronger. I should feel all *I am woman hear me roar* because I defended myself today, but I don't feel an ounce of that. I feel drained and empty. I feel discouraged and idiotic. I feel like he doesn't want me because I'm weak and powerless.

And yet, I feel whole for the first time in a long time while I'm in his arms.

"Get some rest, baby. I'm not going anywhere."

I curl my fingers against the warm skin of his chest, take a deep breath letting his scent invade my mind, and I drift off to sleep. The nightmare that was powerful enough to leave me cold and broken doesn't bother me again.

***

If there were ever a sight in this world I'd want to get used to, it would be Quinten shirtless standing in his kitchen. His tan skin is a stark contrast to the mostly white décor, his dark beard making his eyes shine the brightest blue I've ever seen.

His smile matches mine when he notices me, and I'll be damned if he doesn't do one of those sneaky flexes I've noticed men do around Parker to accentuate the muscles in his stomach.

Blame it on my hormones or the restful sleep I got last night in his arms, but I don't look away from him as I cross the room.

"Pulling out the big guns?" I tease as I reach for a cup in the cabinet, frowning when I notice everything is shoved to the back of the shelf. There's literally no way for me to reach what I need.

I look over my shoulder, noticing a smile he tries to hide behind his own cup of coffee.

"Did you move all of this?"

He shrugs. "Maybe I want you to need me."

More like I need *him* to want *me*—for more than a quick romp between the sheets.

"Can you grab me a coffee mug, Mr. Tree?"

He chuckles, placing his own cup on the counter before closing the distance between us.

"You can get it yourself," he says, close enough that I can feel the heat of his body against my back. Goosebumps race down my arms and tighten my nipples in the most delicious way.

I open my mouth to argue, but he wraps his huge hands around my hips and lifts me. I freeze, suspended in front of him before I realize his intent and reach my hand to the back of the cabinet to grab a mug. The glide back down to the floor has my back and ass running the length of his front. He groans, and I nearly lose it when I feel his erection press against me. I want to stay pinned against him for eternity, and that thought really stresses me out. Wanting something I can't have is painful, a blow not only to my ego but to my self-esteem as well. Regardless of how things end between us, I want to enjoy the ride as long as I can.

"Quinten," I whimper as he releases me, but when I turn around to suggest we do something about that problem in his sweats, he's walking out of the room.

"We're heading to the police station in an hour. I'm glad you're in a better mood."

I'm left standing in the kitchen, no longer needing a cup of coffee to wake me up.

Was he teasing?

Does he want me to follow him to his room?

Is a good time all he sees me as?

I hate being this unsure about everything.

I'm ready in forty-five minutes, but it's the full hour before Quinten reappears from his bedroom. When he does, he barely makes eye contact, even though his hand finds my lower back on the way to the elevator. He stands at my back like a massive guardian on the ride down and I'm so focused on the heat of that huge hand that I don't notice the other person in the garage.

"Parker," Quinten says, forcing my eyes up.

My brows furl as I see my best friend unlocking her car.

"Hey. What's going on?"

"I... umm... I was coming to see you, but I just got called in early for work."

Quinten chuckles, a low rumble from his chest making me realize that he's pressed to my back with his arm around my lower stomach.

"Coming to see me?" I know immediately it's another lie. Her hair is a mess, finger-combed instead of brushed to sleek perfection like usual. Her clothes are wrinkled, making it pretty evident that this is probably the second day she's been wearing them. Her eyes are tired, unfocused, and refusing to meet mine head-on.

Parker loves to have a good time and I begin to wonder if she's in trouble. If she's using drugs or tangled up with a married man or something as equally morally questionable.

"After what happened yesterday..." she says. "Are you okay?"

"What? But I didn't—"

Her phone starts to ring. "I have to go, Hayden. I'll call you later."

In a blink, she's pulling out of the parking spot and driving away.

"That was weird," I mutter, my eyes looking up at the number space she was in. "I'll tell her that these spots are reserved. I don't want whoever is in number twelve-ten to have her towed if she parks there again."

Quinten chuckles again as he guides me to his truck. "I get the feeling he wouldn't mind."

I turn my head to ask who it is, but then his hands are back on me, his fingers lingering in a way that nearly leaves me breathless as he lifts me into the cab. He lingers in the open doorway. His mouth is so close and level with mine and I lean in closer when he begins to close the distance. If the man is toying with me, trying to get me revved up for another round back at his condo, it's working. My body is fully on board. My mind is the only thing I can't get right. I'd give myself over to him fully if I had any assurances that being with me for more than sex was what he wants.

"Seatbelt, Hayden," he says, right before I hear the click of it sliding into place.

"Right," I all but pant as he steps away.

The man is seriously driving me crazy. My body doesn't know which end is up.

The ride to the police station is quiet, the only sounds are the world happening around us. Neither of us reach for the radio buttons or open our mouths to make small talk.

We walk into the police department, me a little timid and scared, him with so much confidence people don't even look his way because he has the air of belonging around him.

The woman at the front counter smiles, her eyes trailing from his face and starting to angle lower when he clears his throat.

He's succinct in his request for a police officer I've never heard of, which isn't a surprise because I don't make a habit of needing police help. The only personal interaction I've had with the police was when my house was broken into.

The officer, or detective I should say with the way he's dressed— more business casual than in uniform—walks up to him and shakes his hand.

"Hayden, this is Detective Jason Augley. Augley, Hayden Prescott."

He shakes my hand as well, and I don't miss Quinten's eyes on the contact as if he's trying to judge the man's intent through the two business-like pumps before releasing me.

"Follow me."

Dutifully, Quinten and I follow the detective through the building until we get to a small, sterile-looking room.

"This can't be done somewhere more comfortable?" Quinten asks the second he gets a look at the interrogation room.

My hands begin to shake, and once again I wonder how much trouble I'm in. I know people can't just get away with shooting others.

"Do you plan to sit in while I talk to her?" Detective Augley asks in a bored tone as if he already knows the answer.

"Of course," Quinten snaps. "Is there a reason you don't—"

Augley holds his hands up as a laugh slips past his lips. "My office is the size of a postage stamp, Lake. We wouldn't fit in there. Have you looked in the mirror lately? You're fu—freaking big, man. I'm just looking out for your comfort." The detective turns to look at me. "I'm just taking your statement. You're not in trouble or in custody. You're free to leave at any time. If at any point you feel uncomfortable, just say so."

I give the man a nod and a weak smile. Even with his assurance, I still feel like a criminal as we enter the room and take our seats.

"First, we're going to talk about what happened. After, I can either have you write it down for your statement, or I can have one of the clerks type it up from the tape and you can come back and sign it."

"Whichever you prefer," I offer, trying to be helpful, but the very last thing I want to do is show up here twice.

"Handwritten is always best," Detective Augley says. "Now, let's get started."

He asks questions and I answer, just like I thought was going to happen, but he doesn't take an accusatory tone or try to catch me in a lie. I relay exactly what happened, and I'm doing well until I have to talk about the moment the guy's gun came out. I'm unable to get through that part without shaking and keeping my eyes dry.

Quinten clasps my hand in his but remains silent. He doesn't try to interject or tell me to breathe when I get a little out of sorts at the end, and that brings me more comfort than he could possibly know. He doesn't discount my emotions. He lets me feel them, lets me work my way through them.

"All done?" Augley asks as he steps back into the room. He gave me time to write my statement.

I sign my name at the bottom with him showing me how to initial in different spots so nothing can be added to the document later.

"I can't tell you much about the investigation, but please know that we haven't apprehended everyone involved. I highly suggest not returning to your house until we do."

"Okay."

"If that's a problem, the Feds can arrange a safe house for—"

"She's staying with me," Quinten snaps, his arm going around my back once again.

Augley smiles. "And that's probably the safest house in the city."

Tell that to my heart.

"Thank you for your time," I tell him.

"If you remember anything else or have questions..." Augley says, handing me his business card.

I take it and nod, letting Quinten guide me out of the police station.

Chapter 31

Quinten

"That was exhausting," Hayden mutters once we're both inside my truck.

"I need to run by the office to take care of a few things, but I can drop you off back at—"

"I'd love to see where you work," she says, a tiny smile playing on her lips.

I get distracted at the sight of them until I have to clear my throat when I realize I'm staring.

"It won't take long," I assure her as I pull into traffic.

"Will Jude be there? Or Wren?"

I clench my jaw. "Probably both. Why?"

I see her shrug from the corner of my eye as my hands tighten on the steering wheel. "It's just more comfortable to be around people I've already met."

I relax a little, but that doesn't stop my mind from wandering back to the night at the bar and Parker trying hard to get Jude and Hayden to notice each other in a romantic way. The woman flirted with me all damned night, and I couldn't see anyone else but the woman in my truck right now. In truth, I haven't been able to see anyone since she gave me attitude over the phone when I called to welcome her back to class along with her flirty friend.

Something shifted recently because I have Hayden with me, and Parker's car was in Jude's spare spot this morning in the garage. I make a point to ask my best friend just what the hell is going on when I get a chance, but that concern is secondary to the woman with me now.

"This office is filled with a group of characters," I warn after opening the passenger door for her. "They're probably going to give me a hard time."

"For what?" she asks, her hands automatically going to my shoulders when I reach to help her out of my truck.

"Could be anything but know that we're family. Blackbridge is home, and even though I may want to throttle them on occasion, I trust each of them with my life. You can do the same."

She nods, her fingers toying with the tiny hairs at the base of my skull as I lift her out of the truck. I'm reluctant to release her, but I get the feeling she wouldn't be okay with me carrying her into the office.

My heart warms when she doesn't hesitate to tangle her fingers with mine when I reach for her. Who knew something as casual as holding her hand would make my heart race and my cock thicken?

I'm making a statement walking into the office with her like this. I'm declaring something before I even have all the answers, and I pray as we climb onto the elevator that I don't end up eating crow.

"Pam, this is Hayden Prescott. Hayden, Pam. She runs the office, and we wouldn't survive without her."

Pam offers my girl a quick smile, but then the phone rings, and she gets back to work.

"Know that Brooks flirts with anything that breathes," I mutter to her as we head toward the breakroom. "And don't be fooled by Finnegan's accent."

"Okay," she says with a slight chuckle. "Is it British? I totally have a thing for British accents."

I look down at her, smiling at the teasing glint in her eyes. "Flynn is the one with a British accent. Finnegan is Irish."

"You're safe then," she says.

"Good to know." I give her fingers a little squeeze as we enter the room. Conversation stops when we step inside. "Don't any of you assholes actually work around here?"

Ignacio looks up, smiling, and it makes me realize I haven't seen him in a while. I give him a little nod, a way of telling him we need to catch up and a lot has happened in the last two months. He nods back in understanding.

"Everyone, this is Hayden Prescott. Hayden," I sweep my arm out to indicate all the smiling assholes in the room, "this is everyone."

"What this idiot means," Brooks says as he stands from the sofa and crosses the room, "is I'm Brooks Morgan."

I barely stifle a growl when he bends down and tries to kiss the back of her hand. I don't know if it's for my benefit, but she yanks her hand back before his lips can meet her skin.

"Would you stop?" Jude snaps, popping his hand against the back of Brooks's head. But then he gets close to signing his own death warrant when he steps up to Hayden and wraps his arms around her. "How are you doing?"

She lets this happen, and I smile when she gives him a few awkward pats on the back, her eyes looking in my direction filled with questions.

"I'm good," she answers when Jude takes a step back.

"Hayden!" Wren yells from across the room because of course he has to be the center of attention.

Hayden screeches, ducking low when Puff Daddy flies out of Wren's office, swooping low toward her before landing on the back of one of the couches.

"Hey, baby," he squawks, his wings spreading wide to show himself off.

"Stop," Kit says, swatting at the bird.

"Listen here fucker," Puff says as he spins around to face Kit. "I'll eat your fucking eyes. I swear I will!"

Kit shakes his head before looking at Hayden. "I'm Kit. This asshole is Puff Daddy."

"I can introduce myself," the bird says. "Come here, pretty lady. Let Daddy get a look at you."

A wide grin spreads across her face, and once again the damn bird is able to charm someone of the fairer sex.

"This explains so much," she whispers as she continues to watch the strutting bird. "After what I heard last night, I thought Wren had a weird—"

"I fucking told you about keeping it down," I hiss at Wren, having a pretty good clue what Hayden heard coming from their apartment last night.

"Sorry," Wren mutters.

"What happened to his—" She points as if she doesn't want to offend the bird.

"Hey, lady! I'm right here. Ask me to my beak!"

Most people would take a step back at the aggression the dumb bird is showing, or they would laugh awkwardly and defer to Wren, but Hayden takes a step closer. "It's nice to meet you, Puff Daddy. What happened to your tail feathers?"

"Just what that damn bird needs," Flynn mutters as he walks into the room. "A captive audience."

"You noticed?" Puff says, holding his wing over his eyes as if he's embarrassed. "I've been attacked. Give me a hug. It helps with the trauma."

Hayden opens her hands, walking closer, and I manage to grab her before she gets too close. "He'll bite your nipple. It's a trick."

Her hands immediately go to her chest, making all the guys in the room laugh. Her cheeks turn bright red as she looks up at me.

"Cockblock!" Puff screams. "Come on, baby. Just a little nibble. I promise you'll enjoy it."

The damn bird starts opening and closing his mouth making sucking noises.

"Wren," Deacon snaps as he enters the room. "Get that bird out of the breakroom. We've talked about this."

"Fucking tyrant!" the bird yells, but he flies back to Wren's office on his own.

"At least he didn't shit on you this time," Flynn tells our boss. "Hi, I'm Flynn Coleman."

Hayden shakes his hand. "Hayden Prescott."

"Nice to meet you. This tyrant is Deacon Black, the big boss."

"The owner of the company," he corrects, holding out his hand as well. "Nice to meet you. Quinten, can I speak with you for a moment?"

"I'll be right back. You okay?" I ask before walking away.

"Don't worry, big guy," Jude says with a clap on my back. "I've got her."

I glare at my friend before walking away, a warning in my eyes.

"You seem like you're in a better mood," Deacon says as we near the coffee pot.

I grunt, not feeling very jovial at the moment. Hayden laughs, the sound drawing my attention back to her, and I don't know exactly how to feel about watching her laughing with my friends.

"That's what I'm talking about," Deacon says pointing to my face. "That smile. It isn't something we see a lot of around here."

I resist the urge to touch my face for verification, but I know it's there.

"I don't know where we're heading," I explain, knowing he'll understand I'm talking about the thing crackling between Hayden and me.

"I know exactly where you're heading, and if I had to guess, I'd say you're already there."

I grunt again, and he laughs as we watch everyone circle around Hayden in the middle of the room.

"What did you need to speak to me about?" I ask, already wanting to go back to her side.

None of the guys are flirting with her that I can tell, but there's an ache deep inside of me that wants to be by her side whenever another man is near. I want to mark my territory and growl at each one of them. I want to bite Jude's hand off when he touches her arm. The animal need to show each one of them that she's mine begins to stir wildly in my gut.

"Yep," Deacon whispers. "Already there. Don't hurt anyone."

He laughs as he walks away, and I get the distinct impression he just proved a point by making me take a step away from her and watch everyone else with her.

"Oh, hey."

My eyes snap to the entrance of the room, finding Parker standing there with a weird look on her face.

"I just wanted to see how you were. I was a jerk this morning."

Jude's spine stiffens as his eyes land on Hayden's friend, his throat working on a swallow before looking away.

Chapter 32

Hayden

"What are you doing here?" I ask Parker as she approaches.

"I wanted to apologize for acting weird this morning." Her eyes stay locked on mine, and it's unusual for Parker not to smile and look around the room when she enters. She's always quick to get her bearings.

Walking into a room filled with good-looking men and not smiling at each one of them is the strangest thing to witness.

"Is there some place we can talk?"

I look to Jude in question, but his eyes are locked on his feet.

"Come on," Flynn says. "You ladies can use my office."

We follow Flynn down a hallway, and I make sure to look at Quinten before walking out of the room. He gives me a slight nod before his attention goes back to the men on the other side of the room.

Parker gives me a weak smile once the door is closed and we're alone.

"What's going on?"

"I should be asking you that," she says, wrapping her arms around me in a hug. "I can't imagine experiencing what you've been through. Are you okay?"

She takes a step back, her hands still on my shoulders as she looks down at me.

"I'm so confused," I admit. "What are you—"

"I saw that look the hot teacher gave you. So, are you two like a thing now? I knew he had the hots for you. I'm glad everything is working out."

"We're... umm..." I brush a strand of hair behind my ear. "I don't exactly know what we are."

"And what exactly happened at your job yesterday?"

I shake my head, unsure that I can talk about it again. I spent an hour and a half going through every detail with Detective Augley, and it has left me completely drained.

"It was so bad," I confess, my emotions starting to get the best of me. "I showed up to work and a strange man was there with Mr. Harrison. It's like the guy knew me, and I'm pretty sure he's the one who broke into my house or is involved with the person who did."

"That's terrible, Hayden."

"He thought I found something I wasn't supposed to. I saw in his eyes that he had no intention of letting me out of that office alive. He took my phone and smashed it. I would've called you, but I haven't had much of a clear head since yesterday."

The truth is my mind has been on Quinten since he brought me back to his place. I shift on my feet hating that the echo of him inside of me has already faded.

"It's fine," she assures me. "Go on."

"Quinten got me a gun. The stubborn man tried to convince me that I won it at the gun range, but I'm not an idiot."

"He's taking care of you. That's a good sign."

"He's trying to fix my problems. That's what he does. I'm just a problem to solve," I confess. "When my problems are gone, he's going to—"

"That man wasn't watching you just a minute ago because he's trying to fix you, Hayden. That man is in love with you."

My heart jolts, wishing it were true, but knowing it isn't.

"He feels obligated to make sure I'm okay."

"That may be true, but I don't think it's for the reason you suspect. He had freaking hearts in his eyes as we walked away."

"You're probably confusing it with annoyance. I've taken over his condo. I'm sure he's counting down the damn days until I go back to my own house."

"You can come stay with me," she offers.

"No," I answer immediately. "I... umm... they haven't caught the other guys involved. The one I shot was only the middleman."

"And there's no opportunity for great sex at my apartment. How was the sex, by the way?"

"Amaz—" I clamp my mouth shut as her smile grows.

"I knew it! Good for you. Great sex solves so many problems." She looks away. "And can cause even more."

"Is there something you need to tell me?"

She shakes her head, her eyes coming back to meet mine as if she's forcing herself to not look suspicious. I grab her hands in mine. "Listen, if you're in trouble, I'm here."

"There's no trouble," she vows. "You're the one with the exciting life right now. All I've been doing is working."

"You're lying."

She frowns.

"I know when you're lying, and you've been doing it for weeks. Is it drugs?"

Her head jerks back. "I'm not on drugs."

"You looked exhausted this morning. I don't think I've ever seen you so disheveled. If you're addicted to—"

"It's not drugs," she repeats.

"But it's something."

"I didn't come here to talk about me."

"You say you came here to talk to me, but how exactly did you know I was here? How did you know where Quinten lived since you were at his building this morning?"

She looks away, her eyes blinking rapidly.

"You're seeing a man there," I surmise. "God, Parker, tell me he isn't married."

Her eyes snap back to mine. "I'd never. You know that. Not after what my mom went through. I could never be the other woman."

"You're addicted to a man." She swallows. "Is he a good guy? Tell me he's not a criminal."

She huffs. "There's no guy."

"Are you in trouble?" I ask again, hating that she's refusing to open up to me. We tell each other everything. Or at least we did until recently. I'm not innocent in this either. I haven't been as forthcoming with her about what I feel for Quinten. Opening my mouth and confessing those feelings will make everything real, and that will only make the pain in my chest worse when it's over.

"It's stupid and I don't want to talk about it."

"But you're here to get help?"

"I'm here to talk to you," she insists.

"You didn't know I was going to be here. I saw that in your eyes when you walked in. Are you here to hire Blackbridge?"

"I'm—" She gives me a weak smile. "Things are fine. Are you sure you're okay?"

I sigh, praying she'll open up when she's ready. If I keep hounding her, it's only going to take longer for that to happen. Parker has always been stubborn, and I let the subject drop because honestly, I have a lot going on right now as well, and I can only focus on my own issues.

"I'm okay. Being around Quinten helps."

"He seems like a nice guy."

"Jude is really nice, too," I say, thinking the shy, quiet man would be great for my friend. If anything, maybe he'd be able to get her to slow down in life.

"Who?"

I tilt my head to the side.

"Jude, the man you studiously avoided looking at when you walked in. You know what? Never mind." She's too distracted right now to listen to anything I have to say.

Her phone chirps with a text. "I have to go, but I hate leaving you."

"I'll be fine," I assure her as I walk toward the closed office door.

"Because you have Quinten," she adds.

I give her a wry smile. She has a lot more faith in that situation than I'm able to muster myself but arguing the point right now isn't the time.

We leave the office, agreeing to get together once this situation blows over. I smile when I look up and see Jude walking our way.

"Jude, you remember my friend Parker."

Parker holds her hand out to him. "Parker Maxwell."

"Jude Morris," he says with a sly grin on his face that makes a million questions come to mind. "But we hug around here."

I take a step back as Jude pulls my friend against his chest, and the hug I'm witnessing looks nothing like the one he gave me. The man is smitten with my friend, his hand a little low on her back for an acquaintance who just pretended like they've never met before. The entire situation is suspicious.

"We'll talk soon," Parker tells me after she steps back from Jude. "Text me your new number once you get your new phone."

She gives a little wave over her shoulder as she walks away. Jude watches her, and I watch him.

"Want to explain that?" I ask him once he realizes he's been staring.

"Is she single?"

I frown at him. "Parker will always be single."

He frowns, giving me a little nod before walking away.

I don't waste time in the hallway. My body urges me back to the breakroom to find Quinten.

Chapter 33

Quinten

"Like I've told every other one of my men when they've found themselves in this situation, take as much time as you need. You're important around here, but we can manage without you for a little while."

I frown at my boss. "What do you mean *in this situation*?"

"Completely in love of course."

Deacon's smile isn't teasing. He isn't fishing for a confession. The look on his face says he's one hundred percent sure about my emotions. How does he know when I'm just discovering them for myself?

"I don't know what you think—"

"Stop before you say something untrue. Take the time off."

I stand from the chair opposite of his desk and leave his office.

Flynn's office door is open, indicating that Parker has left, and my blood heats as I prowl toward the breakroom looking for my girl.

If Deacon is right, and I get a fluttery feeling in my gut that he does for Anna, then I need to talk with Hayden. I need to lay it all out and see where she stands. This dancing around each other, especially after the intimacy we shared yesterday, is ridiculous. We're adults, and we should be able to talk about what we're feeling and what our expectations are. I may have to tone mine down because I'm not sure she'd be keen on the idea of moving in with me and staying naked in my bed twenty-four-seven, but that's exactly where my head was at when I requested a few days off.

Finding her is easy. She's sitting on one of the sofas talking with Flynn and Ignacio. The clench of my fists calms slightly knowing that both of those guys are in committed relationships to the point that they won't even flirt with her in an attempt to get my hackles up, unlike Finnegan and Brooks who see messing with people as an Olympic sport.

"Ready to go?" I ask her the second I step into the room.

"Sure," she says, telling both of the guys goodbye.

Her eyes are on mine as she draws closer to me, and I don't know if it's my own obsession with her or actual heat in her gaze, but my body begins to respond immediately.

The guys chuckle as we leave the room, and it makes me press against her back just a little harder on the way to the elevator. Pam gives us a little wave as we walk through as she continues her conversation on the phone.

She doesn't put any distance between us on the elevator ride down, and she seems reluctant for me to step away when I help her into the truck. Both of those are great signs going into the conversation I know we need to have when we get back to my place.

I don't offer to stop and get food. If she's hungry, we can order delivery, but the longer I put off this talk, the more I'll lose my nerve. Part of me is telling me to take things slow and let whatever it is between us progress at a natural speed, but being with her only for her to pull away the next day is bound to drive me insane. The other part of me is urging me to start the conversation at the first red light we come to.

I manage to keep my lips clamped closed on the drive back, and still in the elevator on our way up to my condo.

She gives me a weak smile when I open the door and indicate for her to step inside. She doesn't pause as she crosses the threshold as she walks toward the guest bedroom.

"Hayden." She stops in her tracks, but I need more than just her attention right now.

In a flash, I have her back pressed to the front door, and I smile as she blinks up at me. When her tongue licks at her bottom lip, I nearly drop the conversation we need to have in favor of stripping her naked right here in the entryway.

"We need to talk."

Her eyes flash with something I can't explain, and I brush my lips against hers to make the uneasy look fade away.

"I fucking yearn for you," I confess as her fingers tangle in the fabric of my shirt at the shoulders.

"Good sex does that to a person."

My cock thickens with the reminder.

"I want to fix all of your problems. It's been hell holding back and watching you try to do it all on your own."

Her teasing smile fades away.

"Fixing things is what I do," I continue. "But I've had to force myself to take a step back. I know you want to work through the problems on your own. I've been fighting it since I met you. I hate seeing you struggle."

Her eyes lock on mine.

"I felt physical pain watching what was happening to you on that video feed. I've never felt terror like that in my life. I feel like I've been put on this earth to protect you, Hayden. I never want you out of my sight, and I know at times that's going to seem a little smothering, but I just can't see myself acting any differently." I swallow, trying to force down the emotion clogging my throat because the tears burning the backs of my eyes don't feel very manly. "I want to pull you to my side and protect you, cocoon you from anything bad that threatens to touch your life. I know you're independent, and I'm in awe of that side of you, but I want to be a part of your bubble."

"My bubble?" She blinks up at me, her cheeks red.

"This barrier you surround yourself with, daring anyone to cross you. I want inside that protective casing. Let me in. Please, Hayden, just let me be a part of who you are."

Her eyes water, and I back a way a little, thinking I'm crushing her without knowing it, but she clings to my shirt.

"You said you don't date."

"Date?" I scoff. "I don't want to date you, Hayden. I want to be a staple in your life. I have no baggage, no real reason to have avoided relationships as long as I have, and as corny as it sounds, I feel like I've been waiting for you, and I didn't even know it. Being inside of you the other night was absolute euphoria, but this isn't just about sex. It never was."

"Waiting for me?"

"For you." I run my nose up the side of her neck, smiling against her skin when her breath hitches. "I want to spend every second with you. I want to make you coffee in the morning and run my hands down your soapy body in the shower. I want to argue with you about stupid TV shows and whether tomatoes are a vegetable or a fruit. I want to pull you to my side and growl at any man brave enough to approach you."

"And sex?"

"Oh, I want lots of that, but not more than you can take." I give her a wicked smile as I pull my face back to gaze down at her. "But I can admit that watching you walk a little funny after being inside of you last night made my cock hard all over again."

"I can't feel you there anymore." She bites her lower lip as her eyes sparkle. "I miss it."

She squeals in delight as I pick her up and carry her to my bedroom.

"No more sleeping in the other room."

"The bed is really comfortable," she argues as she pulls her shirt over her head.

My hands are working my belt open, and I have to pause at the sight of her perfect tits encased in lace. "You drive me wild."

"You need to go grab a condom," she urges, and my feet are immediately carrying me to the guest bedroom to grab that stupid basket Wren—or Whitney—took the time to put together last night when I texted my friend with my urgent request.

"Did you see this stuff in here?" I ask, holding up a packaged butt plug.

Her cheeks flame again. "I'm not opposed to playing, but if the intent is to fit you inside there, that's never going to happen. Is that a deal breaker for you?"

"That miraculous pussy of yours is all I need."

"This one?" she asks, shimmying her jeans and underwear down at the same time before spreading her legs.

"That's the one." I dive for her, mouth locking over the spot in question without warning.

I hold her with gentle hands as she squirms under the assault of my mouth, groaning only a few minutes later when she pulses against my mouth. I may need more than just a few days off if every day is going to be like this with her.

"Condom, now," she pants as her fingers finally let go of my head when I come up for air.

"On top," I insist.

She shakes her head. "Take me like this."

"I don't want to hur—"

"You won't cover me with your body and make me yours?"

"Mine," I agree, snapping the latex on my dick before settling over her.

My pulse is raging inside my chest, but as her arms circle around my neck, I manage to slow things down, entering her with one long confident stroke that makes us both sigh into each other's mouths.

I find the end of her with each stroke, enjoying the way she whimpers as I stretch her. Her fingernails dig into my back, and I know I'm going to have to resist walking into the office and showing the guys that badge of honor.

"Jesus," I pant when her eyes squeeze closed. "Am I hurting you?"

Her head shakes violently. "I'm trying not to come."

"Come, baby. Don't hold back."

"If I do, then you will, and then it'll be over. I want it to last for—oh God!"

Her core clamps down on me, and just as she predicted, her orgasm sets off my own. I bury my face in her neck, push my cock as deep into her as I can, and explode.

Her hands are trembling on my back, legs shaking against my hips, and she gives me the sweetest little smile when I finally manage to pull my head back and look down at her.

"I can't wait to do that again," I whisper.

"A million times," she agrees with a smile big enough to light up every dark corner in my life.

Chapter 34

Hayden

"Would you stop," I hiss with no malice as I look over my shoulder.

Quinten watches me walk into the kitchen from the sofa, an eager erection standing proudly between his thighs.

"I told you what that does to me."

I add an exaggerated limp to my steps as I carry our lunch dishes to the sink.

He groans, a husky sound that makes me wet every time.

He looks like he's in pain when I reenter the room.

"I told you this was a bad idea."

"I'm still not seeing a problem."

"Naked lunch isn't a thing, Q."

He smiles at the nickname I've given him.

"The nakedness isn't the problem, it's the restrictions you've placed on us."

"It's not a restriction," I argue. "It's dangerous. Hot wings and sex before a shower don't mix."

"And I told you that I know you had a life before me, but I don't want to hear about the men—"

"And I explained I read it in a book. It's not something I experienced personally, but I have to say, I do love your jealousy." I cross the room to him, leaning in close and pulling back when he tries to lift his mouth to mine. "I played by the rules and washed my hands in the kitchen."

"Yeah?"

I nod. "You know what that means. I can touch but you can't. Hands behind your head."

He complies comically fast, his eyes darting down the length of me, and that gaze has the power to set me on fire despite him giving it to me almost hourly since we locked ourselves away three days ago.

"We need to talk," I whisper, my mouth an inch from his as I reach down and run a single finger down the underside of his dick.

"After," he insists giving his hips a little swivel.

"Now works for me."

I grab a condom from the side table, opening it before rolling it down the length of him.

"I thought we were going to t—fuck, grip me hard. Jesus, baby. That's perfect."

"Mind if I have a seat?" I ask as I straddle his lap, my thighs spread so wide because of his size that I can feel myself opening before I bring the head of his cock to my entrance.

"Are you wet enough for th—Goddamn it, Hayden. Have you been thinking dirty thoughts?"

"My pussy is always wet for you." I slide down just an inch, pulling off of him when he flexes his hips up. "Be still. Let me."

"I'll try," he promises.

I don't know exactly when things shifted, and I was able to say such dirty things to him without wanting to shy away, but I'm definitely learning to open my mouth more often.

"Now about this conversation. I don't want to freak you out."

"You're not pegging me. I don't care about the strap-on Wren put in the basket he had delivered."

I laugh. His friend has been dropping off care packages daily. The first day it was snacks and drinks with electrolytes, but as each day goes on, the baskets we find in the hallway have gotten increasingly more sexual. I teased Quinten about the strap-on this morning.

"I was thinking of something a little more... mmm that's good... permanent."

His arms flex, but he doesn't pull his hands from behind his head. "Yeah?"

"God, you fill me up. Wait, let me—" I groan when I angle my hips forward, a trick he showed me the first night we were together that allows me to take him to the root.

"Keep making those noises, and I'm—fuck, are you—"

His hands find my waist, his hips surging up as I fall apart. "Really? That was fast. My turn."

I cry out in glee as he lifts me and holds me in the air. God, I love how damn big and strong he is.

"Legs over my elbows, Hayden. Fucking hurry."

My body tingles with need despite having just come as I move my legs where he demands them.

"Hold on, baby. Tell me if it gets to be too much."

His mouth finds mine as he saws into me like a maniac.

Our foreheads are together, both pairs of eyes focused on where we're joined, and despite having come together like this more times than I can count the last couple of days, the sight still thrills me, and I'm already planning for the next time.

"Can you come again?" he pants. I nod my head, my body ready to give him exactly what he's demanding of it. "Now, Hayden. Fuck, baby. Do it now."

My fingers dig into his shoulders, but I don't worry about hurting him. Last time I left marks on him, he seemed thrilled.

"Fuck," he moans, his cock kicking inside of me which sets off my own orgasm. "I'll never get enough. Fucking never."

His mouth finds mine, and the conversation I wanted to have with him is forgotten momentarily as he turns, collapsing on the couch with him still inside of me.

"I want you to move in here with me," he says, and I don't pull my face from his neck as his fingers trace hearts down my spine.

"Really?" The question is muffled, but I feel him nod.

"I know it's soon, but—"

I jerk my head back so I can look into his pretty blue eyes, my fingers tangling in his glorious beard. "That's what I was going to talk to you about."

"Yeah? You want to?"

"I want to spend every second with you. Does that make me crazy?"

"If it does, then I should already be institutionalized."

I press my mouth to his, and things begin to turn heated once again. We can't seem to keep our hands off each other, and that makes me a little nervous about the other part of the conversation I have to have with him.

I pull back, leaning in briefly to swipe my tongue over his kiss-swollen lips. He groans, his arms tightening around me.

"I have to go back to work."

He frowns. "No, you don't."

"I got an email this morning. They need me to go back."

"I mean you don't have to work at all."

I roll my eyes, trying to climb off his lap. He keeps his hold on me, but I don't feel trapped. I know if I press the issue that he'll release me. Truthfully, I like being in his arms, even when I know there's the potential to say something completely ignorant.

"Independent, remember?"

"And I was thinking you'd want to just stay naked in my bed at all times."

I pinch his arm, but it doesn't faze him. "I want to work."

"You hate your job."

"I can't just lie around waiting for you to fuck me."

"Make love," he growls, and I smile.

It's the closest he's come to admitting that level of care for me.

"And you're more than welcome to wait naked on the couch. I'd never restrict you to the bed. I wouldn't mind you in the shower a couple nights a week. There's also potential with the bar in the kitchen. I think it's the perfect height for me to suck on that perfect little clit of yours." His hips roll beneath me, and I groan at how ready he is for me again.

"Again?" I pant.

"If you're planning on leaving me, I need to stock up."

He rolls us over, spreading my legs wide.

"I'm going to work, not leaving you."

I watch, eager and ready as he pulls off the used condom, tossing it to the floor before sliding another one down his length.

"Promise me you'll look for another job," he whispers as he lines himself up right where I need him.

"I promise. Slow, I'm tender."

His hips roll, the motion pushing his cock in the slightest bit before sliding back out. He teases me with the head, and I know it's enough to get me there, but my body demands the stretch of all of him.

"I never knew it could be like this. Fuck, Hayden. Tell me it's the same for you."

"It's perfect."

When our lips meet this time, he slows, his arms looping under my shoulders so his fingers can tangle in my hair. I wasn't lying. He's absolute perfection. The way he holds me. The way he makes love to me. The way his arms reach for me at night if I roll over in my sleep.

But tomorrow, we have to let the real world back in. He'd talked about me letting him into my bubble, and I quickly did that, but I can't help but wonder what we'll be like when we let the rest of the world in as well.

With a skilled roll of his hips, I lose all train of thought. The only thing that matters right now is him and me and this life we're starting to build together.

Everything is perfect, and I won't let a damn thing take it from us.

Chapter 35

Quinten

When Hayden's alarm goes off on her new phone, I resist the urge to grab it and smash the damn thing against the wall. It's not because I'm tired. We've gotten plenty of rest between getting to know each other the last couple of days.

No, that sound means we can no longer hide away. Despite numerous appeals in the last eighteen hours, she still insists on going back to a job she hates, saying it would be rude and unprofessional to just quit. I tried reasoning with her, explaining that no one would bat an eye after what happened the last time she was there, but she's going into the office anyway.

"Give me just one more day," I grumble as I press my lips between her shoulder blades.

Being the big spoon to her little one has got to be the most amazing thing in the world.

"Do you really think that's going to work?" she whispers, her voice still rough from sleep, and the hard-on I have pressed against her back throbs at the huskiness of it.

"What?" I tease, giving my hips another roll.

"You know what."

Her stomach twitches as I run my fingers just below her navel. "Are you telling me my morning wood doesn't turn you on?"

She groans, her body shifting a little.

"That I won't find you... look at that, slick and hot. Stay home, and I'll make you come."

"You'll make me come anyway," she whispers, her leg lifting and angling back to rest on mine, opening herself up for me.

"I could stop."

"You won't." And already she knows me so well.

I bite at her shoulder as she lets me work her over, my cock a steel pipe between us.

It doesn't take long for her climax, but it never does. The woman is a jolt of pure adrenaline to my ego.

"Thank you," she pants, her hand patting mine before she climbs out of the bed.

"Really? Are you just going to leave me like this?"

I point to my naked body and straining dick when she tosses me a saucy look over her shoulder.

"You poor thing," she teases. "Be a good boy and get in the shower so I can suck you off."

I scramble out of the bed, nearly tripping and face-planting when the sheets tangle around my feet, but I'm in the shower, water turned on before she enters the bathroom a few seconds later.

She laughs at me as she climbs in with me, and my own lips turn up in a smile, and then my mouth hangs open in awe as she drops to her knees and takes the head of my cock into her perfect little mouth.

***

"Think people will notice that limp you seem to have?"

She glares at me, but there's no fire in her eyes. "I know one way to make the soreness go away."

"But honey," I tell her, wrapping my arms around her in the kitchen. "Then your knees and jaw will hurt all the time. Oomph."

I step back, hand rubbing at the spot on my stomach where she just elbowed me.

"So violent."

"Keep it up, mister," she says, pointing her coffee spoon at me in warning. "You have thirty minutes to get ready. No stalling. I'm going to work and will get an Uber if I think you're dragging your feet."

I wrap my arms around her once again as she turns back to stir her coffee. I press my lips to her neck and breathe her in.

I want to open my mouth and tell her how happy I am that she's here, how much I'll miss her while we're apart, but I just can't. I don't want to scare her by going too fast. Knowing I'll have a million chances in the future to express my feelings, I press a quick kiss to her cheek before stepping back and popping my hand against her perfect ass.

She glares at me over her shoulder as I walk away and blow her a kiss before ducking down the hallway. I know she's serious about taking an Uber, so I dress quickly.

"Are you nervous?" I ask as we head in the direction of her work twenty-five minutes later.

"I'm terrified, but I figure I just need to rip the Band-Aid off, you know?"

"There's nothing wrong with just taking a little more time. I know I've joked about you staying home forever, and I know that isn't going to happen, but it hasn't even been a week. What you experienced is traumatic. I can't believe the people at your job are making you come back."

"I'm going to look for a new job. I'll probably start on my lunch break today, but Chance Harrison was the bad apple at the company, not everyone else. I hate leaving them in a lurch because of his greediness. There's no telling what kind of mess I'm going to be dealing with. I wouldn't be surprised if the FBI isn't there going over all the records with fine-tooth combs." She looks out the window as downtown St. Louis rolls past. "I may not even have a job soon. I don't imagine the government is going to be very trustful of ViCorp after what happened last week. They may pull all contracts. The company won't survive without those."

"Everything will work out the way it's supposed to," I assure her, but in the back of my mind, I can't help but hope they actually do get shut down. I hate the idea of her showing up to a place and having to look at the office where she was scared for her life. She isn't the type of woman that would ever get hard to something like that. It's going to hurt her in a year as much as it's going to hurt her today, and I want to protect her from that. But once again, this isn't something I can fix for her.

"You'll call me if you need me?"

"I will," she quickly agrees, her hand meeting mine on the console.

I give her fingers a quick squeeze. "I can always go up with you, and growl at anyone who dares to approach you."

"Tempting," she says with a quick roll of her eyes as we pull into the parking garage of her building.

"Kiss me for the world to see, baby." I lean across the console toward her, and she doesn't waste a second meeting her mouth to mine.

She seems as reluctant to pull away as I am, and I cup her cheek in my hand, thumb skating over the dampness on her lips.

"Think about me."

"All day," she promises.

I climb out of the truck and go around to her side, wedging myself between her legs before she can jump down.

"Can't wait to take these off of you tonight," I say as my hands run up her legs to her waist.

"Promise?" she teases as I pull her to me, letting her feel just how excited I am to see her again as I lower her feet to the ground.

"Skip work," I plead one more time.

Her palm presses to my face, and I know I have my answer.

She holds my hand, walking me back around to the driver's side door of my truck like I'm a pouting child. She stands, hands clasped in front of her with an eyebrow raised until I climb back inside.

"Have all of your work done by four forty-five," she insists.

I tap my hand to my forehead. "Yes, ma'am. What's for dinner?"

"Me," she says with a wink, and I love her just a little more when her eyes dart around and her cheeks turn pink.

She heads into the building, and I'm such a fool for her that I watch her in the side mirror of my truck, so entranced by the swing of her hips in those silky fucking pants that it takes too long for my brain to register the dark sedan pulling up.

Tires screech as they pull up beside her, and I know I'm going to hear her scream every time I close my eyes for the rest of my fucking life as she's yanked into the fucking car.

Chapter 36

Hayden

All instincts I ever thought I had fail me when rough hands literally snatch me up, pull me inside a car and throw me without care against the opposite door. I don't reach for the door handle to escape. My fingers immediately go to the pain at the back of my head instead of kicking at the masked man that settles into the seat beside me.

I stare at him in shock, mouth hanging open as he slaps the back of the seat in front of him, urging the driver to get them the hell out of there. I can only see the parts of his face not covered by a ski mask when he looks through the back glass to gauge what Quinten is doing. I curl in on myself, sure that my man is going to shoot out the fucking windows and rescue me.

Surely this isn't happening. Women don't get taken outside of their jobs in broad daylight moments after kissing the man that she loves goodbye, and not after spending the most amazing four days planning their future.

I lift my leg when the car bounces out of the parking garage, the scrape of the underside echoing inside around us.

"Kick me and I'll cut your fucking foot off," he growls. "I'll send you back to that motherfucker in pieces."

I believe him, lowering my leg and whimpering when he reaches for me again. I have no clue what to do. I've read that you fight and do everything you can to not be taken to a different location but seeing as the car we're in is already speeding away from my office building, we're a few steps past that.

My thoughts race to my gun, but the police still have that from the shooting. I know that this is somehow related to all the stuff that happened with Chance Harrison. My body begins to tremble at knowing that these guys came back to finish the job, and now they're going to be angry that I hurt one of their friends.

"Come here," he hisses, and I cringe when he forces me to my front so he can tie my hands at my back. The rope that he's using hurts more than the cuffs the cops clamped on my wrists a few days ago. "Stupid bitch. Ruining fucking everything."

Next, the world disappears behind a blindfold. These guys must have really planned this out because I can't see so much as a splinter of the sun through the dark fabric.

"You shot my fucking brother," the guy growls in my ear, jerking me back to him when I try to cringe away.

"He was going to kill me!" I scream.

"And if he dies, that's still going to happen."

"Quit fucking around with her, asshole," the guy from the front hisses, and it makes me wonder if he's got a decent bone in his body. Maybe I have someone who won't be as quick to— "She's gonna fucking die, regardless. We have our orders."

And there goes that thought.

"She's shaking like a leaf," the guy says with maniacal joy in his voice. "I bet she pisses her pants before we get there."

"I'll cut her fingers off one by one," the guy in the front seat snaps.

I'm trembling so hard, my teeth are clattering together like I've been dropped off naked in the middle of Antarctica, and honestly, if that were the case, I'd probably have a better chance of survival than the situation I'm in.

"Sit back and relax, bitch. We'll be there before you know it."

I don't know where there is, but the ominous threat of it makes me hope they drive for hours.

I start to try to track the direction we're going, counting left and right turns by the pressure the car puts on my body, but we could be driving in fucking circles for all I know.

Tears leak from my eyes, wetting the blindfold, my nose leaking snot I'm unable to wipe away as I sob as quietly as I possibly can.

I'm not a religious person by any stretch of the imagination, but prayers race through my head as the car continues to move.

He mentioned dying if his brother dies, and since that hasn't happened in the last couple of days since being shot, I have no idea how long these guys plan to keep me. Will it be quick and painless if I cooperate? The outcome seems like it's going to be the same, but I can't imagine being tortured slowly, or oh God, what if they plan to sell me to someone? I don't think I'd want to survive if that happens. The guy up front said I was going to die, and as the car bumps along, I try to come to terms with that.

The sobs get worse, shaking my shoulders as I think of never being able to look in Quinten's eyes ever again, of never being able to run my fingers down his beard or fall asleep with the sound of his strong heart beating in my ear.

I'll never get married or have babies.

I'll never find out what the hell is going on with Parker.

I'll never get the chance to tell Quinten that I love him.

I'll die, and he'll never know. He deserves to know.

But maybe it'll be easier for him if he doesn't. Maybe he'll avenge my death, and that thought nearly destroys me as I think of these guys ending his life the way they plan to end mine. I can't fathom a world where he doesn't exist, no matter if I'm long gone from it or not.

"Would you quit that shit?" A rough hand shoves me, forcing me to fall over on the seat, my head once again hitting the door. Pain radiates behind my eyes. "You're giving me a headache."

I shift away as much as I can, pressing my body against the door and curling in on myself. I hate that I'm such a coward, that all of the bravery I had was used up shooting a man I'd only seen once. I curse Chance Harrison to hell for bringing this down on me. I shouldn't be anywhere near this situation.

I should be curled up in bed with strong arms holding me tight. I should be making future plans and looking for a new job, or hell, taking Quinten up on his offer of not having to work at all.

The car begins to slow, and it ramps up the chatter in my jaw. Every muscle in my body is sore from the terror rushing through my blood, and when the car comes to a complete halt, I want to scream. I can't find the courage to do that.

The second the driver's door is yanked open, so is the one at my side, and I fall out of the car, my shoulder roaring in pain when it meets concrete.

"Stand up, you stupid bitch." Rough hands yank me from the ground, and I hate my size for the millionth time in my life. I hate how small I am and how that seems to give people the urge to literally jerk me around.

Angered, I attempt to twist out of his grasp, but I can't. Despite my mighty will, my strength is no comparison to his.

"Nice try, bitch," he growls in my ear. "I'm just gonna put this bitch down right here and get video so Mr. Pierce knows that it's done."

I cry out again when I'm shoved to my knees, and everything seems to calm. Something is pressed to the back of my head, and I hear a click, the sound I'm now familiar with having spent so much time recently at the gun range.

This is it. This is the end.

My eyes have been wide open even though I have a blindfold on, but now I close my eyes, my lips moving in prayer. I whisper my love for Quinten out loud for the first time. I ask God for forgiveness for wasting my life until recently. I pray for strength for the people who care for me. I pray that Quinten is able to move on even though the thought guts me. I pray that Parker finds true happiness and resolves whatever it is she's been struggling with.

And then the shot rings out, and death isn't as painful as I've imagined.

Death is noisy and a flurry of activity, and as I fall face first on the ground, I don't even feel the concrete against my face. I smile, grateful that discomfort is a thing of the past, but then hands grab at me, and I realize I didn't die, and he must have missed.

Now is the time to fight. I roll my body as best I can, the strong arms on me pulling away for a second before grabbing me again. I snap out at them, teeth bared and feeling feral. I won't give up. I won't leave Quinten to find someone else. I can't. Things aren't supposed to be this way. Life isn't so fucked up that you find love only for it to be yanked away.

"Hayden! Hayden. Baby, stop. You're going to hurt yourself."

I'm so fucking beyond people telling me what to do. I pull against the ropes at my back, but strong arms wrap around me from behind. Although I'm no longer on the ground, I'm in no better of a position when I'm lifted off the ground.

"Jesus, fuck!" someone hisses when my foot makes contact with something in my scramble to get away.

Pain radiates all the way up my leg, but I keep on kicking.

"Fuck, dude, are you okay?" the man holding me asks, his voice rumbling through my body.

"Both," someone moans. "She got both my balls."

"I'll kill you!" I roar, wiggling until the guy behind me holds me tighter, making it impossible to move.

"It's Jude," I hear in my ear. "Calm down and let Quinten take the blindfold off."

"You're okay, baby. Listen to my voice. Hayden, do you hear me? It's over."

The fight leaves me in an instant, my arms and feet dangling loosely.

Sunlight nearly blinds me when the fabric is pulled free of my face, and I begin to sob the second my eyes are able to focus on Quinten. His face looks as wrecked as I feel.

"Baby," he whispers, his arms open to me the second Jude lowers my feet to the ground. I don't have the strength to stand and Quinten seems to understand because he's right there to catch me before I fall.

The ropes are untied from my wrists, and although both arms scream in pain, I wrap them around my man, crying uncontrollably into his shirt. He lifts me, my legs going around his waist, but we don't get far.

His face is buried in my neck as he falls to his knees on the hard concrete. Both of our bodies jolt with the force, but we don't stop holding each other.

"I love you," I blurt, because I don't want to live another second without him hearing it from my lips.

"Fuck, baby." He pulls back, his face stained with tears. "I love you, too."

"I was so scared," I sob.

"Me, too."

He pulls me to his chest once again, and when he holds me too tight, making it nearly impossible to breathe, I don't even complain. I never want to be out of his arms.

Sirens blare around us, and we just ignore all of it for long moments.

When we do finally pull away, I see one guy prone on the concrete, face pointed to the sky with unseeing eyes, and another man face down with his hands cuffed behind his back.

I cringe when I see Brooks, a guy I met days ago at the Blackbridge office with a pained expression on his face and a hand covering his pelvic area.

"I didn't mean to hurt your friend."

Quinten shakes his head like it doesn't even matter as his strong hands cup both sides of my face.

"No more work," he says.

"No more," I agree.

"Marry me."

"Of course."

"Soon," he demands.

"Tomorrow," I agree without hesitation.

Chapter 37

Quinten

"You may now kiss the bride."

The small crowd roars, the sound echoing around us in the hotel ballroom as I dip my angel and press my mouth to hers.

I smile against her lips, a promise of all the things to come before my eyes flutter closed and I kiss her for real.

Hoots and whistles fade away, and I'm seconds from ripping her pretty dress off when a throat clearing reminds me that we're in public and getting busy with an audience will never be my thing.

Hayden's cheeks are fire-engine red when she blinks up at me.

"Scandalous," Parker whispers as she hands Hayden back her bouquet of flowers.

Hand in hand, I walk my new bride down the aisle, scooping her up and carrying her into a dark, quiet room off to the side of the ballroom.

"Now?" She giggles as I dig through the twelve hundred layers of her dress.

"Told you I was going to need inside of you the second you became mine."

"I've been yours for a while," she whispers, her fingers scrambling to find the hidden zipper of my tuxedo pants. "Did I tell you just how sexy you are in a suit?"

"Yes," I whisper against her lips as I position myself at her entrance. "Thirty minutes before the ceremony, right before you dropped to your knees insisting on sucking the nerves right out of me."

The bare head of my cock is already leaking with anticipation.

"God, I love your dirty mouth." She gasps, her jaw hanging open when I slide inside of her. "Open for me, baby. That's it. Legs up high. Fuck, I love how tight you are for me."

"Quinten," she moans. "I can't be quiet. Everyone will know what we're—mmm."

I smile against her mouth, hips moving my cock in and out of her.

"You made me wait," I remind her.

"We had sex this morning... twice."

"To marry me," I clarify. "You made me wait."

"Three weeks. Only three—I'm going to come. Shit. I'm going to—"

I cover her mouth with mine, swallowing her breathy moan as her internal muscles begin to ripple down my cock.

"That's it," I praise. "Milk me dry."

I pulse inside of her, my seed unrestricted for the very first time, and let me say, it was so worth the wait.

"I'm going to do that every day for the rest of your life," I promise, my lips making a trail down her neck.

"Prom—"

I clamp my hand on hers when the door to the room opens. I'm not concerned about getting caught, but I also don't want my new bride to be embarrassed.

"Shh," I whisper in her ear, knowing we're tucked away in the middle of three towers of stacked tables and chairs. We won't be seen unless someone is actually looking for us or turns on the light. It's not like I can exactly hide my frame very easily.

"This has to stop," a woman hisses.

A familiar chuckle rings out around the room, and my ears perk up.

"I have to stop? I'm not the one seeking you out, Parker."

Hayden freezes under me, and all of my suspicions since we ran into Parker in the parking garage at my building weeks ago are confirmed.

Hayden hasn't mentioned her friend other than Parker has been distant lately, so I never opened my mouth to voice my own concerns.

"Nothing to say? If you don't want to keep this up, then stop showing up at my condo in the middle of night." Even in the darkness, I can see a large shadow stalk toward another smaller shadow, their outlines lit only by the *EXIT* sign above the door. "I'm not pursuing you. It's the other way around."

"Like I'd ever—"

Her words are cut off with a kiss that makes my body respond only because we're not supposed to be witnessing it.

A slap rings out, and Parker pushes back out of the door just as Jude's hand touches a spot on his cheek.

"Oh my God," Hayden hisses into my palm.

A slow smile spreads across Jude's face as he straightens the lapel on his suit jacket before leaving the room.

"That explains so much," Hayden whispers even though we're now alone in the room.

"I think you should lie down," I tell her.

She slaps at my chest. "We have guests, you big oaf."

"Knees to your chest for thirty minutes," I insist playfully.

"Later," she says with her hand out. "Give me your handkerchief."

I pull the fabric from my pocket and pass it over, my cock going rigid again at the sight of my wife wiping my cum from between her legs.

"Really?" she asks as I begin to stroke up and down my length.

"Always."

"Fine. Once more, but then we have to go dance."

I don't waste another second getting inside of her.

***

The return to our wedding reception is met with knowing eyes, more than one slap on the back, and a couple of winks.

Hayden and I dance and eat and have a blast, and every second that ticks by is another chance for me to fall in love with her all over again. And I do, over and over and over.

I'm smiling like a fool, my hands locked at my own elbows as I hold her up to me while we dance. It's the only way to kiss her and promise her the world without having to bend in two.

"People are staring at us," she says against my lips.

"They're supposed to," I remind her. "It's our wedding day."

I hear, "Oh shit!" and I spin us around to the other couple dancing beside us.

I've been trapped in Hayden's gaze all night, but I'm still very much aware of what's going around us. I've vowed to keep this woman safe, and I plan to keep that promise.

Deacon is staring at the floor in shock. Anna's fingers are gripping the front of his jacket.

"Holy crap, Hayden. I'm so sorry," my boss's wife says as she looks up at us.

"For going into labor?" Hayden smiles wide. "Best wedding gift ever."

"We need to go," Deacon whispers. "The umm... to the umm..."

"Hospital," Jude says as he walks up. "How far apart are the contractions?"

"Don't know," Anna says. "I've been feeling a little weird all day, but no real pain yet."

"Well, the breaking of the amniotic sac puts everything in high gear. Have you been doing the perineal massage? This could be bad if not."

"I will hang your corpse from the office ceiling," Deacon growls, finally out of his trance and glaring at my best friend.

"There he is," Jude says with a wink. "Let's go have a baby."

THE END

Heroic Measures is next in the series!

Synopsis

Opposites don't just attract.
They captivate.
They entice.
They beckon.
As the medic for the Blackbridge Security team, he was just fine hanging out at the office in his spare time.
Jude Morris was...*boring*.
He didn't need excitement.
He wasn't a thrill-seeker.
Then he met a woman who was.
Parker Maxwell, the only woman able to captivate, entice, and beckon him, was his antithesis.
The up to his down.
The light to his dark.
The hot to his cold.
He couldn't take his eyes off of her.
She didn't seem to notice him.
It's going to take heroic measures for this guy to win the girl.

OTHER BOOKS FROM MARIE JAMES

Newest Series
Blackbridge Security
Hostile Territory
Shot in the Dark
Contingency Plan
Truth Be Told
Calculated Risk
Heroic Measures
Sleight of Hand

Standalones
Crowd Pleaser
Macon
We Said Forever
More Than a Memory

Cole Brothers SERIES
Love Me Like That
Teach Me Like That

Cerberus MC

Kincaid: Cerberus MC Book 1
Kid: Cerberus MC Book 2
Shadow: Cerberus MC Book 3
Dominic: Cerberus MC Book 4
Snatch: Cerberus MC Book 5
Lawson: Cerberus MC Book 6
Hound: Cerberus MC Book 7
Griffin: Cerberus MC Book 8
Samson: Cerberus MC Book 9
Tug: Cerberus MC Book 10
Scooter: Cerberus MC Book 11
Cannon: Cerberus MC Book 12
Rocker: Cerberus MC Book 13
Colton: Cerberus MC Book 14
Drew: Cerberus MC Book 15
Jinx: Cerberus MC Book 16
Thumper: Cerberus MC Book 17
Apollo: Cerberus MC Book 18
A Very Cerberus Christmas
Cerberus MC Box Set 1
Cerberus MC Box Set 2
Cerberus MC Box Set 3

Ravens Ruin MC
Desperate Beginnings: **Prequel**
Grab it for free HERE**!**

Book 1: Sins of the Father
Book 2: Luck of the Devil
Book 3: Dancing with the Devil

MM Romance
Grinder
Taunting Tony

Westover Prep Series
(bully/enemies to lovers romance)
One-Eighty
Catch Twenty-Two

Made in United States
Orlando, FL
12 April 2022

16770393R00114